D0448290

The Flying CLASSROOM

The Flying CLASSROOM

ERICH KÄSTNER

Translated by Anthea Bell • Illustrated by Walter Trier

PUSHKIN CHILDREN'S BOOKS

Pushkin Children's Books

71–75 Shelton Street, London WC2H 9JQ

The Flying Classroom was first published in German as *Das fliegende Klassenzimmer* in 1935 by Atrium Verlag AG, Zürich

Text and illustrations © 1935 Dressler Verlag, Hamburg

English language translation © Anthea Bell 2014

This translation first published by Pushkin Press in 2014

0 0 2

The translation of this work was supported by a grant from the Goethe-Institut which is funded by the German Ministry of Foreign Affairs

ISBN 978 1 782690 56 6

Set in Berling Nova by Tetragon, London

Proudly printed and bound in Great Britain by TJ International, Padstow, Cornwall on Munken Pure 120gsm

www.pushkinchildrens.com

Contents

Chapter Three

Fridolin's return · A discussion of the most unusual form captain in Europe · Mrs Egerland's next annoying visitor · A mounted messenger comes to parley on foot · Unacceptable conditions · A workable plan of battle, and No-Smoking's even more workable suggestion

Chapter Four

Single combat ending with a technical K.O. · The boys from the town school break their word · Egerland is torn between two duties · Martin's mysterious plan of action · Several faces get slapped in the cellar · A small heap of ashes · Permission to win the snowball fight · And Egerland stands down as leader of the town boys

Chapter Five

The boys run into handsome Theodor again · A discussion of the boarding house rules · Unexpected praise · A suitable punishment · The housemaster's long story · And what the boys said about it afterwards

Chapter Six

A painting of a coach-and-six · An old joke goes down well · Balduin as a first name · A damp surprise · A ghostly procession · Itching powder sprinkled by a weird apparition · Johnny on the window sill and his plans for the future

Chapter Seven

A description of Professor Kreuzkamm · A hair-raising incident · The sentence that the boys have to write out five times · Uli's strange announcement in break · A walk with Dr Bökh · A meeting at the allotment · And a handshake beside the fence

Chapter Eight

Contains a lot of cake · The next rehearsal of The Flying Classroom *· Why Uli brought an umbrella with him · Great excitement on the sports field and in the school building · Dr Bökh says comforting things · Martin reads his letter in Piano Room 3*

Chapter Nine 107

Chapter Ten 119

Chapter Eleven 131

Chapter Twelve 142

Afterword 151

Foreword Part One

*A discussion between Mrs Kästner and her son ·
The peak of the Zugspitze mountain · A butterfly
called Gottfried · A black and white cat · A little
of the eternal snows · A pleasant evening after
work · And a farmer's professional opinion that
calves sometimes grow up to be big bullocks*

This is going to be a real Christmas story. In fact I meant to write it a couple of years ago, and then of course I meant to write it last year. But you know how it is; something was always getting in the way. Until my mother said, only the other day, 'If you don't start writing this minute, you won't get anything for Christmas!'

That made up my mind for me. I packed my case at top speed, putting in my tennis racket, my bathing trunks, my green pencil and enormous amounts of writing paper, and when we were standing on the railway station concourse, sweating and feeling harassed, I asked, 'Where do I go now?' Because, understandably enough, in the middle of a summer heatwave it is really difficult to sit down and write: 'It was bitterly cold, snowflakes were falling from the sky, and when Dr Eisenmayer looked out of the window both his earlobes froze.' I mean, with the best will in the world you can't write that kind of thing in August, when you're lying in the family bathtub feeling like a pot roast and expecting to get heatstroke any moment. Well, can you?

Women are practical. My mother had a good idea. She went up to the ticket office window, nodded to the ticket-seller in a friendly way, and asked, 'Excuse me please, but do you know where snow still lies on the ground in August?'

The man was probably about to say, 'At the North Pole,' but then he recognized my mother, bit back any such sarcastic remark and said politely, 'On the peak of the Zugspitze mountain, Mrs Kästner.'

So there and then I had to buy a ticket to Upper Bavaria where the Zugspitze, the highest mountain in Germany, is to be found. My mother added, 'Don't come home until you've written that Christmas story, understand?' Then the train drew out of the station.

'And don't forget to send your washing home!' my mother called after me.

Just to annoy her a bit, I shouted back, 'Mind you remember to water the flowers!' Then we waved our handkerchiefs until we were out of sight of each other.

So now I've been staying for the last two weeks beside a large, dark-green lake at the foot of the Zugspitze mountain, and if I'm not swimming or doing exercises or playing tennis, or getting Karlinchen to row me out on the lake, I sit on a little wooden bench in the middle of a wide meadow, with a table that keeps on wobbling in front of me, and I am writing my Christmas story on that wobbly table.

Flowers of all colours grow around me. Tall, quaking grass bows respectfully to the wind. Butterflies flutter through the air, and one of them, a large peacock butterfly, even visits me now and then. I've christened him Gottfried, and we get on well together. Hardly a day goes by without his settling confidently on my writing paper. 'How's things, Gottfried?' I ask him. 'Is life still fun?' He opens and closes his wings gently by way of an answer, and flies happily on his way.

Someone has stacked up a big woodpile on the outskirts of the dark wood of fir trees. A black and white cat crouches on it, staring at me. I strongly suspect her of being a magic cat who could talk to me if she wanted. She just doesn't want to. Every time I light a cigarette she arches her back.

In the afternoon she goes away, because then it's too hot for her on top of the woodpile. It's too hot for me as well, but I stay where I am. Sitting like that, boiling hot, and writing about a snowball fight, for instance, is no mean achievement.

Then I lean far back on my wooden bench, I look up at the peak where the cold, eternal snows shine in the mountain's rocky ravines—and I find that I can go on writing! On many days, to be sure, clouds come up over the part of the lake where bad weather is brewing, and they drift across the sky towards the mountain peak, towering up until I can't see it any more.

Of course that makes it impossible for me to go on describing snowball fights and other definitely wintry activities, but it doesn't matter. On such days I simply write about indoor scenes. An author has to get bright ideas like that.

In the evening, Eduard regularly comes to fetch me. Eduard is a brown calf with tiny horns, and he's as pretty as a picture. I can hear him coming, because he has a bell hanging round his neck. First it is heard from far away, for the calf grazes in a mountain meadow high above, and then the sound of the

bell comes closer and closer. Finally Eduard comes into sight. He steps out from among the tall, dark-green fir trees, with a few yellow marguerite daisies in his mouth as if he had picked them specially for me, and he trots across the meadow until he comes to my table.

'Hello, Eduard, time to stop work for the day?' I ask him. He looks at me and nods, and his cowbell rings. But he goes on grazing a little longer, because beautiful buttercups and anemones grow here. And I write a few more lines, while high above an eagle circles in the air, rising up and up into the sky.

Finally I put away my green pencil and pat Eduard's warm, smooth coat. And he nudges me with his little horns to remind me to stand up. Then we stroll home together over the beautiful, flowery meadow.

Outside my hotel we part company, because Eduard doesn't live at the hotel, but with a farmer round the corner.

The other day I asked the farmer about him, and he said yes, Eduard would certainly grow up to be a great big bullock.

Foreword Part Two

The loss of a green pencil · The size of children's tears · Little Jonathan Trotz and his ocean voyage · Why his grandparents didn't meet him · In praise of a thick skin · And the urgent necessity of combining courage and intelligence

Yesterday evening, when I'd eaten my supper and was sitting idly in the hotel lounge, I really meant to go straight on writing. The glow of the Alpine sunset had faded away. The peaks of the Zugspitze and Riffelwände mountains were sinking into the shadows of nightfall, and on the other side of the lake the smiling face of the full moon gazed over the dark forest.

Then I discovered that I'd lost my green pencil. It must have fallen out of my pocket on the way back to the hotel. Or maybe Eduard, the pretty calf, had eaten it, thinking it was a blade of grass. Anyway, there I sat in the lounge, unable to write anything. Because although I was staying in a very posh hotel, there wasn't a green pencil for me to borrow anywhere in the entire place. Oh, wonderful!

In the end I picked up a children's book that its author had sent me, and began reading. But I soon put it down again. The book made me really cross, and I'll tell you why. Its author tries to tell any children who read his book that they are having non-stop fun the whole time, and they're so happy they hardly know what to do with themselves! That dishonest gentleman acts as if childhood were made of the very best cake mixture.

How can a grown-up forget his childhood so entirely that a day comes when he simply doesn't know how sad and unhappy children can sometimes be? (I would like to take this opportunity of asking you, with all my heart, never to forget your own childhood! Will you promise me that? Word of honour?)

For it makes no difference whether you're crying over a broken doll, or maybe, later, because you have lost a friend. It's never a question of exactly what makes you sad but of how much you grieve for it. Heaven knows, children's tears are no smaller than the tears shed by grown-ups, and often they weigh more heavily. Don't get me wrong, ladies and gentlemen! We don't want to be unnecessarily soppy. All I'm saying is that you have to be honest even if it hurts. Honest right to the bone.

In the Christmas story that I am going to tell you, beginning in the next chapter, there's a boy whose name is Jonathan Trotz, although the others call him Johnny. That little fourth-year boy is not the central character of this book, but a short account of his life fits into my story here. He was born in New York, his father was German, his mother was American, and they fought like cat and dog. In the end Johnny's mother ran away, and when he was four years old his father put him on board a steamer setting out from New York for Germany. He bought the boy a ticket for the crossing, he put a ten-dollar note in Johnny's little brown wallet, and he hung a piece of cardboard round Johnny's neck with his name on it. Then they went to see the ship's captain. And Johnny's father said, 'Please will you take my son over the ocean to Germany? His grandparents will meet him when he gets off the ship in Hamburg.'

'That's all right, sir,' replied the captain. And then Johnny's father went away as well.

So the boy crossed the ocean all by himself. The passengers were very kind to him. They gave him chocolate, they read the notice round his neck and said, 'Well, aren't you in luck, going on such a long sea voyage at your age!'

When they had been at sea for a week they arrived in Hamburg, and the captain waited by the gangway for Johnny's grandparents to turn up. All the passengers disembarked and patted the boy's cheeks once again. 'O Johnny,' said a Latin teacher in the vocative, 'may all go well for you!' And the sailors going ashore called, 'Keep a stiff upper lip, Johnny!' Then some workmen came on board, to repaint the ship so that it would look sparkling clean before the voyage back to America.

The captain stood on the quayside holding the little boy's hand, looking at his wristwatch from time to time, and waiting. But Johnny's grandparents never turned up. They couldn't, because they had been dead for many years. Johnny's father, who simply wanted to get rid of the child, had shipped him off to Germany without a second thought.

At the time Jonathan Trotz didn't understand what happened to him. But he grew larger, and there were many nights when he lay awake crying. And he will never in his life really recover from the grief he felt at that time, although you can believe me when I tell you he is a brave boy.

However, a reasonable solution was found. The captain had a married sister; he took the little boy to live with her, visited him when he was in Germany, and when he was ten years old sent him to boarding school at the Johann-Sigismund Grammar School in Kirchberg. (This boarding school, by the way, is the scene of our Christmas story.)

Sometimes Jonathan Trotz still goes to see the captain's sister in the holidays. The family there are very nice to him. But usually he stays at the school. He reads a lot. And secretly he writes stories.

Perhaps he will be a writer one day, but no one can tell yet. He spends half-holidays in the big school grounds, talking to the great tits. They fly down to perch on his hand and look at him inquiringly with their little eyes when he speaks to them. Sometimes he shows them a small, brown wallet and the ten-dollar bill inside it...

I told you the story of Johnny's life only because the dishonest writer whose book I was reading in the hotel lounge last night says children are always cheerful, in fact quite beside themselves with joy the whole time. If only he knew!

The serious business of life begins long before you start to earn a living. That's not where it begins, or where it ends either. I emphasize these well-known facts not to make you feel you're the cat's whiskers, heaven forbid! And I don't emphasize them to make you scared. No, no! Be as happy as you can! And be so cheerful that your little tummies hurt with laughing!

Only don't pretend to yourselves, and don't let other people pretend to you. Learn to look misfortune in the eye. Don't be afraid when something goes wrong. Don't just cave in when you have bad luck. Keep a stiff upper lip. You must learn to be tough and develop a thick skin!

You must be able to stand up to blows, as boxers know. You must learn to take them and put up with them. Otherwise you'll feel groggy the first time life slaps you down. Because life wears a large size of boxing glove, ladies and gentlemen! If life has hit out at you, and you weren't prepared for it, a little housefly has only to cough and it will knock you flat.

So keep a stiff upper lip and develop a thick skin, understand? If you stand up to the first blows of fate, you're well on the way to winning. Because in spite of the blows that you have received, you'll have the presence of mind to activate two very important qualities: courage and intelligence. Remember what I tell you: courage without intelligence doesn't amount to anything, and intelligence without courage is no good either. At many times in the history of the world, stupid people have been brave and intelligent people have been cowardly. That wasn't the way to go about it.

Only when the brave have become intelligent and the intelligent have become brave will we really be sure of something that we often, but mistakenly, feel is an established fact: the progress of mankind.

By the way, as I write these almost philosophical remarks I am sitting on my wooden bench again, at the wobbly table, in the middle of the large and colourful meadow. I bought myself a green pencil this morning in the general store here. And now it's late afternoon again. Newly fallen snow is glittering on top of the Zugspitze mountain. The black and white cat is crouching on the woodpile, staring at me. She must be under a magic spell! And down from the mountain comes the sound of the cowbell round my friend Eduard's neck. He will soon be here to nudge me with his little horns and fetch me home. Gottfried the peacock butterfly didn't visit me today. I hope nothing has happened to him.

And tomorrow, at last, I shall begin writing my Christmas story. It will be about brave people and scaredy-cats, about clever people and stupid people. There are all kinds of children in a boarding school.

I've just thought of something: do you all know what a boarding school is? It's a kind of school where you live as well as having lessons. The boys stay there. They eat at long tables in a big refectory, and they have to lay the tables themselves. They sleep in big dormitories, and in the morning the caretaker comes and pulls a bell rope, and a bell rings very loudly. And a few of the boys from the top class are dormitory prefects. They keep watch like hawks to make sure that the others jump out of bed on the dot. Many boys never learn to make their beds neatly, and so when the others go out on Saturdays and Sundays they stay in the boarding house writing lines. (Not that the lines teach them how to make their beds.)

The parents of the boarders live in cities far away, or in the country where there are no secondary schools. And the children only go home in the holidays. Many boys would like to stay at home when the holidays are over. Others would rather stay at school even in the holidays if their parents would let them.

And then there are other students who are day-boys. They live in the town where the school is, and they don't sleep in its boarding house but at home with their parents.

However, here comes my pretty-as-a-picture friend Eduard the calf, stepping out of the dark-green wood of fir trees. And now he shakes himself and trots right across the meadow to me and my wooden bench. He has come to take me back to the hotel. It's time I stopped writing for today.

He is standing beside me, looking at me affectionately. So forgive me if I stop now! I'll get up early tomorrow morning, and then, at last, I will begin telling the Christmas story.

My mother wrote yesterday asking how far I had got with it.

Chapter One

Climbing the front of the school building · Some sixth-formers practise for dancing class · A form captain who can lose his temper to good effect · A big white false beard · The story of the adventures of The Flying Classroom *· A rehearsal of Johnny's play in rhyme · And an unexpected interruption*

Two hundred stools were pushed back. Two hundred school-boys stood up noisily and made for the refectory doors in a crowd. Lunch at the Kirchberg boarding school was over.

'Oh wow!' groaned Matthias Selbmann to one of the boys who had been sitting next to him. They were both in the fourth form. 'I'm ravenous! I need a few pfennigs for a bag of cake trimmings from the bakery. Got any cash?'

Fair-haired Uli von Simmern got his purse out of his pocket, gave a couple of coins to his friend, who was always hungry, and whispered, 'Here, Matz! But don't get caught. That handsome Theodor is on duty in the garden. If he sees you going out of the school gates you'll be for it.'

'You can trust me to deal with your silly sixth-formers, scaredy-cat,' said Matthias loftily, pocketing the money.

'And don't forget to come to the gym. We're rehearsing again.'

'I'll be there,' said Matz, nodding, and he disappeared to run off as fast as he could to Mr Scherf the baker in Nordstrasse, who sold bags of cake trimmings cheaply.

It was snowing outside. Christmas was coming. You could positively smell it in the air... Most of the schoolboys ran out into the gardens surrounding the school and threw snowballs at each other, or if they saw someone walking down the path, lost in thought, they would shake the trees as hard as they could to make snow fall off the branches. Laughter from a hundred throats filled the school grounds. Some of the sixth-formers, smoking cigarettes and with their coat collars turned up, strode up Mount Olympus with great dignity. (Mount Olympus was the name that, for decades, had been given to a remote and mysterious hill, out of bounds to everyone but the sixth-form boys. Rumour said that ancient Germanic sacrificial stones stood on this hill, and sinister initiation ceremonies were performed there before Easter every year. Scary stuff!)

Other boys stayed in the school building and went up to the living quarters to read, write letters, have an afternoon nap or do some work. Loud music came from the rooms with pianos in them.

Some boys were skating on the sports field, which the care-taker had flooded the week before to make an ice rink. Then, all of a sudden, there was a fierce scuffle. The ice hockey team wanted to train there, but the skaters didn't want to let them have the rink. A few boys from the younger forms, armed with snow shovels and brooms, were cleaning the ice. Their fingers were freezing, and they made angry faces.

There was an excited crowd of children outside the school, all looking up. Because on the third floor, little Gäbler from the lowest form was balancing on the narrow window sills as he made his way over the front of the building from room to room. He was clinging to the wall like a fly, inching his way slowly sideways across the façade.

The boys watching him held their breath.

At last Gäbler reached the end of his climb and, with a single bound, leaped in through a wide-open window!

'Bravo!' cried the spectators, clapping their hands enthusiastically.

'What's been going on?' asked a sixth-former, arriving a little later.

'Oh, nothing special,' said Sebastian Frank. 'We just asked the screech-owl to look out of the window, because Harry didn't believe that the screech-owl squints.' The others laughed.

'Are you trying to pull my leg?' asked the sixth-former.

'I'd never dare, would I?' replied Sebastian modestly. 'Someone your size? If I tried pulling a leg like yours, I should think I'd sprain my wrist.'

The sixth-former decided to walk on fast.

Then Uli came running up. 'Sebastian, you're supposed to be at the rehearsal!'

'The king commands, and I obey!' declaimed Sebastian with mock solemnity, and he set off at a slow trot.

Three boys were already standing outside the gym: Johnny Trotz, the author of the Christmas play that bore the exciting title of *The Flying Classroom*; Martin Thaler, form captain and scenery designer; and Matthias Selbmann, who was always hungry, particularly after meals, and wanted to be a boxer one day. He was munching, and held out a few cake trimmings to little Uli as he arrived with Sebastian. 'Here!' he growled. 'Have something to eat so you'll grow up big and strong.'

'If you weren't so daft anyway,' Sebastian told Matz, 'I'd ask how a clever person can eat so much!'

Matthias, a kindly soul, just shrugged his shoulders and went on munching.

Sebastian stood on tiptoe, looked through the window and shook his head. 'Those demigods are dancing the tango again.'

'Come on!' Martin ordered, and the five boys went into the gym.

They obviously didn't think much of the spectacle that met their eyes. Ten sixth-formers, paired off in couples, were dancing on the wooden floorboards. They were practising for dancing class. Tall Thierbach had borrowed a lady's hat, probably from the school cook. He had perched it on his head at a jaunty angle and was moving as if he were a young lady, with his partner's arm elegantly clutching him round the waist.

Martin went over to the piano, where handsome Theodor was sitting, hitting as many wrong notes as he possibly could.

'Those clowns!' growled Matthias scornfully. Uli hid behind him.

'Please, I must ask you to stop,' said Martin politely. 'We want to go on rehearsing Johnny Trotz's play.'

The dancers stopped. Handsome Theodor stopped playing the piano and said, arrogantly, 'Kindly wait until we don't need the gym ourselves any longer!' Then he went on playing. And the sixth-formers went on dancing.

Martin Thaler, the fourth-form captain, went fiery red. He was well known for going bright red like that. 'Please stop now!' he said in a loud voice. 'Dr Bökh the housemaster said we could rehearse in the gym every day from two to three in the afternoon. You know perfectly well he did.'

Handsome Theodor turned round on the piano stool. 'Is that any way to speak to your elders and betters?'

Uli wanted to run away. He didn't like such difficult situations. But Matthias held him firmly by the sleeve, stared angrily at the sixth-formers and muttered, 'Hey, want me to sock that tall fellow one?'

'Calm down,' said Johnny. 'Martin will settle things.'

The sixth-formers were standing in a circle round the small figure of Thaler as if they were going to eat him. Handsome Theodor began playing the tango again. Then Martin pushed the bystanders out of the way, went up close to the piano and slammed its lid down! The sixth-formers were too surprised to do anything about it. Matthias and Johnny made haste to help Martin, but he could manage without them. 'You have to keep the rules just the same as we do!' he told the sixth-formers indignantly. 'Being a few years older than us doesn't make you special! Go and complain about me to Dr Bökh if you like, but you must get out of the gym at once. I insist!'

The piano lid had come down on handsome Theodor's fingers. His face, usually attractive enough for a photograph, was distorted with anger. 'You just wait, laddie!' he said menacingly. But then he left the gym.

Sebastian opened the door and bowed with exaggerated politeness as the other sixth-formers went away too. 'Those smoochy dancers,' he said scornfully when they had gone.

'Twirling around in dancing class with girls who paint their faces—they think the earth revolves around them. They ought to read what Arthur Schopenhauer has to say about women.'

'I think girls are very nice,' said Johnny Trotz.

'And I have an aunt who's a good boxer,' remarked Matthias proudly.

'Come on!' cried Martin. 'Jonathan, the rehearsal can begin.'

'Right,' said Johnny. 'We'll rehearse the last scene again today. It needs more work. Matz, you haven't quite got the hang of your part yet.'

'If my old man knew I was acting in a play he'd take me away from this school like a shot,' said Matthias. 'I'm only joining in to give you lot a hand. Who else could play St Peter, tell me that?'

Then he took a big white false beard out of his trouser pocket and hitched it over his ears so that it covered half his face.

J ohnny's play, as I have already told you, was to be performed in the gym as part of the school's Christmas festivities, and it was called *The Flying Classroom*. It had five acts, and it was almost prophetic in a way. It set out to show what school might really be like in the future.

In the first act, a teacher played by Sebastian with a false moustache glued to his upper lip flew off in a plane, taking his whole class, to have geography lessons in whatever part of the world they were studying. 'Lessons on the spot itself,' ran a line of verse in the first act. That wasn't Johnny's line, but had been added by Sebastian, who was very clever and hoped to make the teachers laugh when he declaimed it. Martin, the form captain, was good at drawing, so he had done the scenery. An aeroplane painted on white cardboard was fixed to the parallel bars in the gym. It had three propellers and three engines, and a door that you could open to get into the plane (or rather, get to the parallel bars).

Uli Simmern was playing the sister of one of the flying schoolboys. He had got his cousin Ursula to send him a dirndl dress. And they were going to hire a blonde wig with long braids pinned up on it from Krüger the barber. They had been to his barber shop last Saturday when they went out, and had tried the wig on Uli. It made him unrecognizable—he looked just like a girl! It cost five marks to hire the wig, but Krüger the barber had said that if they all promised to come to him to be shaved later, when they needed it, they could hire it half-price, and they all promised that they would.

So in Act One the class set out. In Act Two, the plane landed on the rim of the crater of Vesuvius. Martin had painted the mountain erupting in flames on a big piece of cardboard. It looked alarmingly real. They had only to prop the cardboard in front of a high bar in the gym to keep Vesuvius from falling over, and then Sebastian, as the teacher, could deliver his rhyming lesson about volcanoes, and ask his pupils questions about the Roman cities of Herculaneum and Pompeii that were buried under the lava. Finally he lit a cigar at the flame shooting out of the crater painted by Martin, and then the plane went on its travels again.

In Act Three they landed at the pyramids of Giza, walked past the next painted piece of cardboard scenery, and got Sebastian to tell them about the building of those huge tombs for the ancient Egyptian Pharaohs. Then Johnny, painted as white as a mummy, appeared out of one of the pyramids as Ramses II. He had to bend a bit, because the cardboard pyramid was too small. First Ramses delivered a speech praising the fertile waters of the Nile, and the blessings of water in general. Later he asked how the end of the world, as predicted by his astrologer, was getting on. He was very angry when he heard that the world was still in existence and hadn't yet come to an end, and he threatened to fire the astrologer at once. Uli, playing the part of the girl, had to laugh at the old Egyptian Pharaoh and tell him that the astrologer must have died ages ago. On hearing that, Ramses II made a mysterious sign, and Uli, under a spell, followed him into the pyramid as it slowly closed. Left behind, the others had to be very sad at first, but then they set off once more.

In Act Four *The Flying Classroom* landed at the North Pole. The axis of the earth was sticking out of the snow, and the schoolboys saw with their own eyes that the earth is flattened at the poles. They sent a radio photograph of it to the *Kirchberg Daily News*, listened to a polar bear (played by Matthias wrapped in a fur coat) singing a poetic song about the loneliness of living at the North Pole up there in the snow and ice, they shook the polar bear's paw when they said goodbye, and flew away again.

In the fifth and last act, because of a mistake made by their teacher, causing height control in the plane to fail, they ended up at the gates of heaven. There they met St Peter, sitting in front of a fir tree with candles on it, reading the *Kirchberg Daily News* and celebrating Christmas. He told them that their headmaster, Dr Grünkern, was an old friend of his, and asked how he was. There wasn't much for them to see up here, he said, because heaven was invisible. And they couldn't take photographs either.

The teacher asked if St Peter could get them back the little girl who had been kidnapped by Ramses II and taken into the pyramids. St Peter nodded, recited a magic spell, and Uli promptly came climbing out of a painted cloud! They rejoiced and sang 'Silent night, holy night'.

Then all the spectators, teachers and pupils would sing along too, in celebration of Christmas, and the performance would end happily.

So today they were rehearsing the last act. St Peter, played by Matthias, sat on a chair in front of a painted Christmas tree, and the others—except for Uli, who was still inside the pyramid—stood reverently round him. Matthias scratched his detachable white beard, and sang in a voice pitched as low as he could manage:

> *Boys like you, ten or eleven,*
> *are not allowed to visit heaven.*
> *You fly your modern plane up here,*
> *to look in through a telescope.*
> *But that is neither here nor there,*
> *For views of heaven you cannot hope.*
> *It has high walls built all around,*
> *You see me, yes—and then the ground.*

MARTIN:	*That really is a crying shame!*
SEBASTIAN:	*Well, we won't worry, all the same.*
	We're happy just the way we sound.
ST PETER:	*You can't see heaven until you're dead.*
JOHNNY:	*A photograph would do instead.*
ST PETER:	*No, photographs are not allowed.*

Such things are hidden by a cloud.
Explore what I tell you is suitable,
But you must leave the rest...

Matthias stumbled over the last word. It was too difficult for him, and as he worried about that he forgot the rest of his part. He stared at Johnny the poetic genius, silently apologizing. Johnny went over and quietly prompted him.

'Oh yes. You're right,' said Matz. 'But you see, I'm ravenously hungry, and that always has a terrible effect on my memory.' However, he then pulled himself together, coughed and went on:

	Explore what I tell you is suitable,
	But you must leave the rest inscrutable.
	We know you hate to be forbidden
	To see what has to be kept hidden.
	But there's far more you have to know
	Before such mysteries I show.
JOHNNY:	*St Peter's going rather far.*
	I'll wait until I go to college
	Before amassing all that knowledge.
MARTIN:	*Aiming to be a superstar?*
SEBASTIAN:	*They say that you know everything,*
	St Peter, so do you know whether
	The little girl our friend's alive?
	She followed Ramses to the wild
	Maze of the pyramids together.
ST PETER:	*Oh, poor child!*
	Now let me try to cast a spell
	To bring the lost girl back again

It just might work, though who can tell?
What is past is gone and over,
May she no more be a rover,
Now her steps the path have trod,
Leading you and her to God.
Come with me and...

But at this moment the door of the gymnasium was flung open. Matthias failed to get the next few words spoken by St Peter out of his mouth. The others turned in alarm, and Uli, feeling curious, craned round the painted cloud where he had been waiting to make his entrance.

A boy stood in the doorway. His face was bleeding, and so was one hand. His suit was torn. He flung his school cap angrily to the floor and shouted, 'Do you know what's just happened?'

'No, how could we, Fridolin?' asked Matthias in friendly tones.

'If a day-boy comes back to school after lessons looking as badly beaten up as you,' said Sebastian, 'then I suppose—'

But Fridolin interrupted. 'Never mind all that!' he cried. 'The boys from the secondary school in town attacked me and Kreuzkamm on our way home. They took Kreuzkamm prisoner. And what's more, they stole the dictation exercise books that Kreuzkamm was taking back to his old man to be corrected!' (Kreuzkamm's father taught German at the Johann-Sigismund Grammar School.)

'Oh wow! You mean they've got the exercise books as well?' asked Matthias. 'What a stroke of luck!'

Martin looked at his friend Johnny. 'Are there enough of us?' Johnny nodded.

'Off we go then !' cried the form captain. 'Over the fence to the allotment gardens! And let's get a move on! We'll meet at No-Smoking's place!'

They raced out of the gym. Uli was running along beside Martin. 'If handsome Theodor catches us, we're done for!' he gasped.

'You can always stay here,' said Matthias.

'Me? Are you nuts?' asked little Uli, offended.

The six boys had reached the outskirts of the school grounds. They climbed the fence and vaulted over it.

Matthias still had his fake white beard over the lower part of his face.

Chapter Two

More about the man known as No-Smoking · Three spelling mistakes · Uli's fear of being a scaredy-cat · A council of war in the railway carriage · Fridolin is sent off as a scout · The reason why Rudi Kreuzkamm was attacked · Five boys go jogging

The boys didn't know the real name of the man they called No-Smoking. And they didn't call him No-Smoking because he didn't smoke. In fact he smoked a great deal. The boys went to see him. They visited him in secret, and they liked him a lot. They liked him almost as much as their housemaster, Dr Johann Bökh, and that's saying something.

They called him No-Smoking because there was an old railway carriage that had been taken out of service in his allotment garden, and he lived in it summer and winter alike. The carriage consisted entirely of second-class no-smoking compartments. He had bought it for 180 marks from German Railways when he moved into the garden settlement a year ago, he did some work on it to convert it into a home, and now he lived in it. He had left the little white notices saying 'No Smoking' on the carriage windows.

Wonderful flowers bloomed in his little garden in summer

and autumn. When he had finished planting them out, watering and weeding them, he lay in the green grass reading one of the many books he owned. In winter, of course, he lived in the railway carriage most of the time. He kept his unusual house warm with a little round iron stove. It had a blue-black pipe that stuck up above the roof, and sometimes gave off clouds of smoke.

Johnny was going to see about his Christmas presents. (This year, Johnny was staying at school even for the Christmas holidays, because the captain was on his way to New York.) The boys had clubbed together and had already bought their friend some presents: warm socks, tobacco, cigarettes and a black pullover. They hoped it would fit, but to be on the safe side they had made sure that the shop would change it.

Martin, who had very little money because his parents were poor, so he had a scholarship for half his fees at the school, had painted a picture for No-Smoking. It was called 'The Hermit', and it showed a man sitting in an allotment garden full of brightly coloured flowers. Three boys stood by the fence waving, and he was looking at them with a friendly yet sad expression on his face. Small birds, robins and great tits, perched trustingly on his hands and shoulders, and shimmering butterflies danced in a circle above his head.

It was a lovely picture. Martin had spent at least four hours painting it.

Johnny was going to surprise No-Smoking with these presents on Christmas Eve. They knew that he would be spending Christmas all alone, and they felt sorry about that.

In the evening he always put on his best suit and went into town. He had told them that he gave piano lessons, but although they didn't contradict him they didn't believe it. Rudi Kreuzkamm, who was a day-boy and got around town a good deal, had said that in the evenings No-Smoking played the piano in the Last Bone restaurant on the outskirts of Kirchberg, and he got one mark fifty pfennigs and a hot supper in return. That hadn't been proved, but it was perfectly possible. It didn't matter to the boys. What they knew for certain was that No-Smoking was a nice guy, and clever, and he had probably had a lot of bad luck in life. He didn't look as if he had set out all along with the idea of hammering out hit tunes on the piano in smoke-filled bars.

They had often gone to him for advice before, particularly when they didn't want to consult their housemaster. Dr Bökh's nickname was Justus, which means someone who is always fair. Because Dr Bökh always *was* fair. That was why they respected him so much.

But sometimes they needed advice in cases where it was difficult to tell what was right and what was wrong. Then they didn't dare go to Justus, and instead they climbed over the fence to ask No-Smoking.

Martin, Johnny, Sebastian and Fridolin, the injured day-boy, went through the gate of the bare, snowy garden. Martin knocked on the door, and then they disappeared into the railway carriage.

Matthias and Uli stayed outside. 'Looks like there's going to be a real punch-up,' said Matthias with satisfaction.

And Uli said, 'The main thing is to make sure we get those dictation exercise books back.'

'No, it isn't,' said Matthias. 'I have a nasty feeling I made a ghastly mess of my dictation. Uli, do you spell *provinss* with a double "s" at the end?'

'No,' said Uli. 'It ends with "ce".'

'Oh,' said Matthias. 'Then I got that wrong. How about *prophitabul*? With a "ph" in the middle?'

'No, with an "f".'

'But does it end *bul*?'

'No, it ends *ble*.'

'There I go again,' moaned Matthias. 'At least three mistakes in just two words. That must be some kind of record! I'm in favour of telling the boys from the town school to give us Kreuzkamm back, and then they can keep the dictation exercise books.'

They said nothing for a while. Uli, who was feeling cold, trod from one foot to the other. Finally he said, 'All the same, I'd swap with you any day, Matz. I don't make so many mistakes in dictation, or arithmetic either. But I'd be very happy with your bad marks if I could be as brave as you.'

'That's total garbage,' said Matthias. 'I'm dead stupid and there's nothing to be done about it. My old man can get me as much extra coaching as he likes. I just don't understand that stuff. And to be honest I couldn't care less how you spell *provinss* and *prophitabul* and *karousel*. I'm going to be heavyweight world boxing champion later, and then I won't need to spell. But you can easily stop being a scaredy-cat if you only want to!'

'You have no idea,' said Uli, sadly, rubbing his numb fingers. 'The things I've tried, just to keep myself from being so scared. You simply would not believe it. And every time I make a resolution not to run away and not to put up with what other people say—an absolutely firm resolution! And when it comes to it I'm making for the hills again. It's horrible when you feel the others don't trust you to do anything right.'

'I tell you what, you just have to do something that will make them respect you,' said Matthias. 'Something really terrific. Something to make them think: wow, what a great guy Uli is. We were dead wrong about him all along. Don't you think that's a good idea?'

Uli nodded, bowed his head and kicked the fence with the toe of his boot. 'I'm freezing,' he finally explained.

'And no wonder,' said Matthias sternly. 'You don't eat enough. It's a crying shame! We can hardly stand by and watch. I bet you're homesick as well, right?'

'Thanks, it's not too bad,' said Uli quietly. 'Except sometimes up in the dormitory when they're blowing the Last Post over in the infantry barracks.' He felt ashamed.

'And here am I hungry again already!' cried Matthias, angry with himself. 'I was hungry at dictation this morning, too. I felt like asking old Professor Kreuzkamm if he could lend me a sandwich. Instead I have to bother about working out whether words are spelt with *ph* or *f* or double *s*!'

Uli laughed, and said, 'Matz, do take that big white beard off!'

'Good heavens, am I still wearing it?' asked Matthias. 'Sounds just like me.' He put the beard in his pocket, bent down, made a collection of snowballs and threw them as hard as he could at No-Smoking's chimney pipe. He scored two hits.

T he four other boys were sitting uneasily on the well-worn plush upholstery inside the railway carriage. Their friend No-Smoking wasn't very old yet. Maybe about thirty-five. He was wearing a shabby jogging outfit, leaning against the sliding door, smoking a small English pipe and listening, with a smile, to Fridolin's lengthy report on the attack. Finally the boy came to the end of it.

Sebastian said, 'I think it would be a good idea if Fridolin went straight off to find out from the Kreuzkamms whether Rudi is home yet, and if he brought the dictation exercise books with him.' Fridolin jumped up and looked at No-Smoking, who nodded.

And Martin cried, 'But if Rudi isn't back home, you'd have to tell their maid what it's all about when she answers the door, so that Professor Kreuzkamm doesn't catch on.'

'And then,' said Sebastian, 'you go to Egerland's house, and we'll be waiting here for you. And if the gang from the town school haven't come up with Rudi and the exercise books, we'll climb on Egerland's roof. He'll have been behind the attack, and we must hold on to him—maybe we can take him hostage, negotiate with the other boys from the town and swap him for Rudi.'

'All right,' said Fridolin. 'You know where Egerland lives, don't you? Yes, 17 Förstereistrasse. See you soon, then. Mind the rest of you are there too.'

'You bet we'll be there,' said the others. Fridolin shook hands with No-Smoking—Fridolin's own hand, scratched by the enemy, was still bound up with a handkerchief—and then he raced away. The other boys got to their feet as well.

'Just tell me,' said No-Smoking in his clear, reassuring voice, 'how this Egerland and the other boys from town could have thought up the idea of kidnapping your teacher's son and laying hands on your literary efforts?'

40

The boys said nothing at first. Then Martin spoke up. 'This is a question for someone who's good at writing things. Go on, tell him, Johnny!'

So Johnny told him. 'There's a long story behind the attack,' he said. 'In fact it's almost prehistoric. It's said to have been just the same as much as ten years ago. The quarrel is between the two schools, not the boys there. Really, they're only doing what the history of the schools lays down. On an outing last month, we got a flag away from them in the town playground. A kind of pirate flag with a skull and crossbones on it. We refused to give it back. Then they complained over the phone to Justus, and he tore us off a strip! But we didn't confess to anything. So he threatened that if that flag wasn't back in the hands of the boys from the town school, we couldn't even say hello to him for two whole weeks.'

'Funny kind of threat,' said No-Smoking, with a thoughtful smile. 'Did it work?'

'Like a dream,' said Johnny. 'The boys at the school in town got their flag back the very next day. It was lying in their school yard as if it had dropped from heaven.'

Sebastian interrupted Johnny. 'There was only one snag. The flag was a little bit torn.'

'Rather a large bit torn,' Johnny corrected him.

'And now they'll be wanting to take revenge on the dictation exercise books,' Sebastian, clear-minded as ever, finished the explanation.

'Right, then off you go back to your prehistoric war,' said No-Smoking. 'Maybe I'll look in at the battlefield in Försterei-strasse and treat the wounded. I must just change my clothes first. I like the sound of your housemaster Justus more and more.'

41

'Yes, Dr Bökh is a great guy,' cried Martin enthusiastically.

No-Smoking started slightly. 'What did you say was your housemaster Justus's real name?'

'Dr Johann Bökh,' said Johnny. 'Do you know him, by any chance?'

'I'm not sure,' said No-Smoking. 'I used to know someone with a similar name... well, off you go, get on the warpath, you Hottentots! And don't break anyone's neck. Not your own, and not the necks of the boys from the town school either. I'm just going to put a fuel briquette in my stove to keep it going, and change my things.'

'See you later!' shouted the three boys, and they ran out into the garden.

Once outside, Sebastian said, 'I bet you he knows Justus.'

'It's none of our business,' Martin pointed out. 'If he wants to visit him, well, now he knows where to go.'

They joined Matthias and Uli. 'At last!' growled Matthias. 'Uli's half frozen.'

'Jogging will warm us up,' said Martin. 'Come on!' And they trotted off towards the town.

Chapter Three

Fridolin's return · A discussion of the most unusual form captain in Europe · Mrs Egerland's next annoying visitor · A mounted messenger comes to parley on foot · Unacceptable conditions · A workable plan of battle, and No-Smoking's even more workable suggestion

It was still snowing. The boys' breath formed vapour in the air while they ran, as if they were smoking fat cigars. A few third-formers were standing outside the Eden Cinema on Barbarossaplatz waiting for it to open, so that they could go in and see the film.

'You go on!' Martin called to his friends. 'I'll catch up with you.' Then he went over to the third-formers. 'Listen, you could do us a favour,' he said. 'Never mind the cinema! The boys from the town school have captured Kreuzkamm, and we have to get him out of their clutches.'

'Want us to come with you right away?' asked Schmitz, one of the third-formers. He was small and round, and people called him Little Barrel.

'No,' said Martin. 'There's plenty of time. Can you be in Vorwerkstrasse on the corner of Förstereistrasse in a quarter of an hour? Bring a few more people with you. And put your caps in your pockets, or that gang from the town school will guess what we're up to too soon.'

'That's okay, Martin,' said Little Barrel.

'Can I rely on you, then?'

'You bet,' said the third-formers. Martin ran on, gasping for breath. He caught up with the others, and as they didn't want to be noticed he led them a long way round to Förstereistrasse. They stopped at the corner of Vorwerkstrasse.

A little later Fridolin came racing up.

'Well?' they all asked at the same time.

'Rudi isn't home yet,' he said breathlessly. 'Luckily their maid isn't as stupid as she looks. If the Professor asks, she's going to tell him Rudi was invited to supper at our house.'

'This is getting serious, then,' said Matthias, pleased. 'I'll just pop round to Number 17 and smash Egerland into tiny little atoms.'

'You stay here!' Martin told him. 'Smashing people to atoms is no kind of solution. And if you tear Egerland's head off we still won't know where to find Kreuzkamm and the exercise books. Stick around, we'll soon be needing you.'

'This sounds like a job for me,' said Sebastian Frank, and he was right. 'I'll go and parley with them. Maybe we can do this by negotiation.'

'Oh yes, you look like the person to do that, don't you?' Matthias laughed sarcastically.

'I'll at least find out where Rudi is,' said Sebastian. 'That's worth doing.' He went off. Martin walked a little way with him.

Matthias leaned against a lamp-post, took a notebook out of his pocket and moved his lips as if he were working something out.

Uli was freezing again. 'What are you counting, Matz?' he asked.

'My debts,' admitted Matthias gloomily. 'I'm eating my old man out of house and home.' Then he closed the notebook, put it away again and said, 'Fridolin, lend me a few pfennigs, will you? It's all in a good cause. You'll get the money the day after tomorrow at the latest. My old man wrote to say he's sent the money for my journey home and twenty marks on top of that. If I don't get something to eat I won't be able to hit anyone.'

'That's blackmail,' said Fridolin, giving him ten pfennigs.

Matthias shot off like an arrow from a bow, straight into the nearest baker's shop. When he came back he was munching blissfully, and he held out a paper bag to the others. It contained deliciously crisp and crusty rolls. However, his friends refused the offer. Fridolin was peering round the corner of the street, concentrating hard. And Johnny Trotz was gazing into the window of a grocery shop as if no less than the treasure of the Incas was on display there. The others had seen this before. Whenever Johnny looked at anything, he gave the impression that he had never set eyes on anything like it. That was probably why he did so little talking. He was fully occupied with seeing and hearing things the whole time.

Then Martin turned the corner. However, he just nodded to them, and disappeared into the building on the corner of Vorwerkstrasse. Uli was glad to see Matthias eating with such a good appetite. 'Martin's a great guy, isn't he? Remember how he chucked those sixth-formers out of the gym?'

'Martin is without the shadow of a doubt the most unusual form captain in Europe,' said Matthias, munching. 'He works disgustingly hard, but no one could call him pushy or a swot.

He's been top of the class ever since he came, yet if there's a serious punch-up he's always right in there with us. His parents pay only half the school fees, so the rest is a scholarship, but he doesn't knuckle under to anyone. Whether they're sixth-formers or teachers or the Three Kings of the Orient, if he's in the right he won't give way.'

'I think he's following the example of Justus,' said Uli, as if he were telling a great secret. 'He loves what's fair and right, the same as Justus does. I expect that's how you get to be like those two.'

Sebastian rang the doorbell on the third floor of Number 17 Förstereistrasse, where the Egerlands lived. A woman opened the door and looked at him gloomily. 'I'm in the same class as your son at school,' said Sebastian. 'Can I have a word with him, please?'

'This place is like a railway junction today,' complained Mrs Egerland. 'So much coming and going! What's the matter with you boys? First one of you comes for the key to the cellar so that he can put his sledge away, the next needs a washing line in a hurry, and the rest of you march all over the apartment leaving grubby marks on my carpets.'

Sebastian wiped his boots clean on the doormat and asked, 'Is your son on his own now, Mrs Egerland?'

She reluctantly nodded and let him in. 'His room's along there.' She pointed to a door at the far end of the corridor.

'Oh, and before I forget,' said Sebastian, 'did you get the cellar key back?'

'You want to put a sledge away too, do you?' she grunted.

He shook his head. 'Not necessarily, Mrs Egerland,' he said, and he walked into the enemy leader's room without knocking.

Egerland from the school in town was so surprised that he jumped off his chair. 'What's the idea?' he asked. 'One of the grammar-school bunch!'

'I'm kind of a mounted messenger,' said Sebastian. 'I mean, I'm an envoy, and I've come to parley with you, so please bear that in mind.'

Egerland frowned. 'Then you might at least tie a white hand-kerchief round your arm. Or it'll be the worse for you when my people catch you.'

Sebastian took out a handkerchief, said with a smile, 'It's not all that white any more,' and tied it round his right arm, using his left hand and his teeth.

'So what do you want, then?' asked Egerland.

'We want you to hand over our friend Kreuzkamm from school and our dictation exercise books.'

'What are you offering in exchange?'

'Nothing,' said Sebastian coolly. 'Our people are marching up at this moment, and we'll recapture the prisoner if you don't let him go of your own accord.'

Egerland laughed. 'First you'd need to find out where he is. And then you'd have to set him free. Those two things will take you a lot of time, my dear fellow.'

'I don't want to be on friendly terms with you,' said Sebastian sternly. 'I'm not your dear fellow, understand? And let me point out that there isn't a single thing you can do with Rudi Kreuzkamm. Were you planning to keep him hidden for days on end? That could really land you in trouble. But let's get to the point. What are your conditions?'

'There's only one condition,' said Egerland. 'You must write us a letter, straight away, apologizing for tearing our flag and asking us to give you back the prisoner and the exercise books.'

'Or else?'

'Or else we'll burn the dictation exercise books and keep Kreuzkamm prisoner. I can promise you here and now, he'll grow old in captivity if you don't write that letter! He's getting beaten up, too. A slap in the face every ten minutes.'

Sebastian said, 'Of course your conditions are unacceptable. I'm asking you, for the last time, to hand over Kreuzkamm and the exercise books unconditionally.'

'We're not about to do any such thing,' replied Egerland firmly.

'Then my mission here is over,' said Sebastian. 'We shall proceed to free the prisoner in about ten minutes' time.'

Egerland took a black cloth off the table, opened the window of his room, hung the cloth out of the window and shouted down to the courtyard, 'Hey there!' Then he closed the window, laughed mockingly, and said, 'Go on, free him if you can!'

They bowed coldly to each other by way of saying goodbye, and Sebastian left the apartment as fast as he could. When he got back to his friends, the third-formers, led by Little Barrel, had just arrived. About twenty boys were standing in Vorwerkstrasse, with their feet freezing, waiting for their envoy to return from parleying.

'They want us to write a letter of apology for tearing their flag,' said Sebastian. 'And they also want us to ask, in writing, for the return of the prisoner and the exercise books.'

'What a joke!' said Matthias. 'Come on, everyone! Let's make mincemeat of them!'

'Where's Martin?' asked Uli, sounding anxious.

'And where exactly *is* Kreuzkamm?' asked Johnny Trotz.

'I think they tied him up and then locked him in the Egerlands' cellar,' said Sebastian. 'Egerland's old lady almost said so. They asked her for the cellar key and a washing line.'

'Then here goes!' shouted Little Barrel. And the others could hardly wait.

At this point Martin came running up. 'Come on! They're already gathering in the courtyard.'

Sebastian told the form captain what had happened.

'Where've you been all this time?' asked Uli.

Martin pointed to the building on the corner of Vorwerkstrasse. 'You can see over to the Egerlands' courtyard from there. He hoisted a black cloth out of his window and shouted "Hey there", and now the gang's arriving from all the nearby buildings.'

He looked around at the others, counting. 'There are enough of us,' he said, reassured.

'Do you happen to know where Kreuzkamm's hidden?' asked Sebastian, with a touch of jealousy.

'Yes, in the Egerlands' cellar. With some of the boys from the town school guarding him. We must strike at once, or they'll be getting more and more reinforcements. We'd better storm the courtyard and occupy the cellar. Half of you, under Johnny's command, go into the building from the street. The other half, under my command, climb over the wall from the corner building where I was just now, and get into the courtyard to attack their flank. But a few minutes later.'

'Just a moment,' said someone behind them. They turned in alarm.

No-Smoking was standing there, smiling. 'Good evening!' they all called to him, and smiled back.

'Your plan won't work, of course,' he explained. 'Egerland already has thirty boys there. I looked carefully. And war between you will make such a racket that the flying squad will come out.'

'And then the police will tell both schools,' said Uli, who was freezing-cold again, 'and there'll be a terrible scandal. So close to Christmas, too!'

Matthias looked sternly at his small friend.

'Well, it's true,' said Uli, sounding embarrassed. 'It's not that I'm scared on my own account, Matz.'

'What do you suggest, then?' Martin asked.

'See that building site?' said No-Smoking. 'Challenge the boys from the town school to meet you there, and then settle it by single combat. Why would you all want to fight? You and they should choose a representative each. It's quite enough to have two of you fighting each other. If your man wins, they'll have to hand over their prisoner unconditionally.'

'And suppose their man wins?' asked Sebastian sarcastically.

'Oh, for goodness' sake!' said Matthias. 'Have you gone round the bend all of a sudden? Just let me get another of these crusty rolls inside me.' He reached into his paper bag, and then began chewing. 'The town school people will pick Wawerka. I can beat him with my left hand.'

'Right!' cried Martin. 'Let's try it that way! Sebastian, you go and get them to the building site. We'll go straight over.'

'And make a mountain of snowballs, to be on the safe side,' called Sebastian. 'Just in case anything goes wrong.'

Then he raced off round the corner.

Chapter Four

The grammar school boys were standing on one side of the building site, the boys from the town school on the other. Exchanging nasty looks, they measured each other up. A formal meeting of the two leaders took place in the middle of the site.

Sebastian, as the negotiator, accompanied Egerland. 'Our opponents agree with the suggestion,' he told Martin. 'So we'll decide it by single combat. They're nominating Heinrich Wawerka to represent them.'

'And Matthias Selbmann will be our champion,' said Martin. 'He suggests that the fight will be decided when one of them either leaves the ring or isn't capable of fighting any longer.'

Egerland looked at Wawerka, a tall, sturdy boy. Wawerka nodded with a dark expression, and Egerland said, 'We accept those rules for the fight.'

'And if our champion wins,' announced Sebastian, 'you'll return us the prisoner and the dictation exercise books unconditionally. If Wawerka wins you can keep them.'

'And then I suppose you'll write that letter of apology?' asked Egerland sarcastically.

'Well, at any rate we'll renegotiate,' said Martin. 'In the worst case we'll even write the letter. But the single combat comes first.'

'I will now ask the leaders to return to their men!' called Sebastian.

A clear space was left between the two armies. On the left, Wawerka stepped out of the ranks of the boys from the school in town. On the right, Matthias came forward.

'Here we go, here we go!' chanted the boys from the town school.

'Hooray for us! Hooray for us!' bellowed the grammar school boys.

Now the two champions were facing each other warily. Everyone fell silent, waiting for the hostilities to start. Neither of the boys seemed to want to go first.

Then, quick as lightning, Wawerka suddenly bent down and pulled his opponent's feet from under him. Matthias fell backwards and landed full-length in the snow. The other boy flung himself on top of him and began punching Matthias as hard as he could.

The town boys were yelling encouragement. The grammar school boys were alarmed, and Uli, shaking with fright and the cold, kept muttering to himself, 'Matz, do go carefully! Matz, go very, very carefully! Matz, be ever so, ever so careful!'

All at once, Matthias managed to grab Wawerka's right arm and twisted it, slowly and mercilessly. Wawerka was swearing like a trooper, not that it did him any good. He had to give in and roll over on his side. Then Matthias got hold of Wawerka's head and pushed his adversary's face deep into the snow. Wawerka was flailing his legs about and gasping for breath.

Surprisingly, Matthias let go of him, jumped three paces back and waited for the next attack. His left eye was swollen. Groaning, Wawerka stood up, spat out large mouthfuls of snow and raced furiously towards Matthias. But Matthias ducked, and the boy from town jack-knifed over him—and fell in the snow again! The grammar school boys were laughing and clapping. Matthias turned to his friends and shouted, 'That was just for starters. Watch this!'

Wawerka got to his feet, clenched his fists and waited. Matthias came closer, swung back his arm and hit Wawerka, who hit back. Matthias hit him again, and so it went on for a while. It didn't look as if either of them had an advantage over the other. Then Matthias bent down. Wawerka lowered his fists to protect his body, but Matz shot up again at once and punched Wawerka's unprotected chin.

Wawerka tottered, turned groggily round in a circle, and couldn't raise his arms. He was dazed.

'Go on, Matz!' shouted Sebastian. 'Finish him off!'

'No,' Matthias shouted back. 'I'll let him get his breath back first!'

Wawerka bent over, with difficulty, and stuffed a handful of snow down the collar of his jacket. That revived him. He raised his fists once more and ran at Matthias. Matthias dodged to one side—and Wawerka raced past him. 'Stop, stop!' shouted the other boys from the town school. Wawerka stopped, turned round like a bull in the bullring and growled, 'Come on then, you rotter!'

'Just a moment,' said Matthias. He went closer and held one of his fists under Wawerka's nose. Wawerka hit out furiously. But that left his face exposed again, and before he knew it he had been punched so hard behind his ear that he sat down. He scrambled up again, lurched towards Matthias and got two resounding blows in the face. They weren't really necessary now, because there was no way he could go on fighting. Matthias grabbed the defenceless Wawerka by the shoulder, turned him round and gave him a kick. Like a wound-up clockwork toy, Heinrich Wawerka stumbled out of the ring and into the middle of the speechless group of boys from the town school. If they hadn't stopped him, he would have staggered on and on.

Matthias was applauded enthusiastically by his friends, who crowded up to shake hands with him. Uli was beaming all over his face. 'I was scared, but I stood up to my fright so as to back you!' he announced. 'Does your eye hurt very badly?'

'Not a bit,' growled the winner of the fight, moved by his friend's concern. 'By the way, do you have my last crusty roll there?' Uli handed him the bag with the last roll in it, and Matthias began munching away again.

'Now let's go and get Kreuzkamm!' said Little Barrel.

But it didn't turn out as they had hoped. Egerland came over, looking embarrassed, and said, 'I'm terribly sorry, but my men don't want to give the prisoner back.'

'That won't do!' protested Martin. 'We discussed it all before the fight. You lot can't just break your word!'

'I entirely agree with you,' replied the downcast Egerland. 'But they're refusing to do as I say, and there's nothing I can do about it.'

Martin was looking angry again. 'This is incredible!' he cried, beside himself. 'Don't they have any sense of decency?'

'Wow, if only I'd known that,' said Matthias, still munching, 'I'd have made minsemeat of Wawerka. Uli, how do you spell minsemeat?'

'With a c in the middle,' said Uli.

'Right, I'd have made mincemeat of him with as many cs as you like in the middle,' said Matthias.

'I feel really bad about this,' said Egerland. 'I do agree with you, but I have to stand by my men, don't I?'

'Of course,' said Sebastian. 'You've had bad luck, that's all. You're a typical example of conflicting duties. That kind of thing used to happen a lot in the past.'

No-Smoking strolled slowly over the building site, gave Matthias an appreciative nod and asked what was going on.

Sebastian told him.

'Good heavens!' said No-Smoking. 'Are there really fellows like that around today? Martin, I'm sorry I suggested the single combat to you. It's a good way of settling quarrels, but only between decent people.'

'You're dead right there, sir,' said Egerland. 'All I can do is offer myself to the grammar school as a hostage. I'm your prisoner, Martin Thaler!'

'Well said, my boy,' remarked No-Smoking. 'But of course there's no sense in that. How many more boys are going to end up behind locked doors today?'

'That's all right,' Martin, his face pale and serious, told

Egerland. 'You're a good sort. Go back to your men and tell them we're going to attack in two minutes' time. And that will be the last fight ever between you and us, because we don't go fighting people who break their word. We despise them instead.'

Egerland bowed in silence and walked away.

Martin hastily assembled the boys and said quietly, 'Now, listen hard! In two minutes' time I want you to start a full-scale snowball fight—or at least a fight with plenty of snowballs. I'm putting Sebastian in charge, because Matthias, Johnny Trotz and I are going on a little excursion, and mind you don't win the snowball fight before we get back! It's your job to keep the boys from the town school busy here. You can even retreat a bit if that helps, so that they'll keep coming after you.'

'I don't understand your idea,' said Little Barrel. But he bent down and made snowballs.

'That's a good plan,' said Sebastian appreciatively. 'You can rely on me, Martin. I'll keep things lively here.'

Uli, who would have liked to stay with Matthias, went up to Martin. 'Can't I come with you too?'

'No,' said Martin.

'Uli,' called Sebastian, 'you have to stay here and help us retreat. You're really good at that!'

Tears came to Uli's eyes.

Matthias took a swing as if to flatten Sebastian. Then he growled, 'Another time. I don't want to get personal now.'

The first snowballs were flying through the air. Sebastian gave his orders. The battle of the building site began.

'Chin up, young man,' No-Smoking told Uli. He nodded to the others. 'Best of luck, you lot. You've got Martin, you don't need me.'

'You bet!' they shouted back. Then, looking thoughtful and friendly, No-Smoking walked through the storm of snowballs and went home to his railway carriage.

Sebastian was going from group to group. The grammar school boys, furious because the town boys had broken their word, could happily have knocked them all down. Little Barrel was particularly impatient. 'Why don't you give the order to—' charge them, he had been going to say, but an enemy snowball hit him right in the mouth. He looked taken aback. The other third-formers laughed.

'I knew you didn't see why we mustn't win at the moment,' said Sebastian. 'But you have to do as we say all the same.' Then he looked round for Uli, whose hands were freezing, so he had put them in his pockets. When he saw Sebastian looking his way, he quickly took his fingers out again and joined in the bombardment.

Meanwhile Martin, Johnny and Matthias were running down Vorwerkstrasse. They disappeared into the house on the corner, ran into the yard there, got over the wall and reached the gate to the yard of the building where Egerland lived.

'There's the cellar door,' whispered Martin. Matthias cautiously unlatched it, and the three of them silently climbed down the slippery steps. It was pitch-dark, and the cellar smelled of old potatoes.

Now they were groping their way along low-ceilinged, narrow passages. They turned corners from time to time. Then Johnny tugged at Martin's sleeve. They stopped, and saw a side corridor where a light showed. Slowly they crept closer, and heard the voice of a boy they didn't know.

'Kurt,' said the voice, 'that's another ten minutes up.'

'We'd better get back to work, then,' said another strange voice. 'My hands are hurting.' And now they heard a loud slapping noise six times in succession. Then it was silent as the grave again.

'What surprises me most is that you're not ashamed of yourselves,' said a third voice all of a sudden.

'That's Kreuzkamm,' whispered Johnny. And they crept slowly on until they had a good view of the scene. Two boys from the town school were standing behind a wooden door that had been left ajar, and Rudi Kreuzkamm was sitting on an old, wobbly kitchen chair. He had a washing line wound all round him so that he couldn't move his arms and legs, and his cheeks were unnaturally red. Three candle ends were burning on a table. And there was a Christmas tree leaning against the wall in the far corner, among wood, briquettes and coal. Egerland's father had bought it two days earlier.

'I'll shout to attract attention as soon as my friends have set me free,' said Kreuzkamm furiously.

'You'll have mouldered away by then,' said one of the town boys.

'They'll have found out where I am within an hour at the latest,' retorted Kreuzkamm confidently.

'You'll still have plenty of slaps ahead of you,' said the other boy. 'Six every ten minutes, that makes thirty-six in all.'

'Applied mathematics!' cried the first boy, laughing loud enough to make the low-ceilinged cellar echo. 'Or maybe your friends will turn up before that, do you think?'

'I hope so,' said Kreuzkamm.

'Then we'd better slap your face another six times now to be on the safe side. Payment in advance. Make yourself useful, Kurt!'

The town boy called Kurt went up to Kreuzkamm's chair, raised his left hand and slapped Kreuzkamm's face. Then he raised his right hand, hit Kreuzkamm and said, 'That makes two.' He raised his left hand again—but by then Matthias was beside him, and the third slap went into Kurt's own face.

He crashed into the Egerlands' Christmas tree, got stuck among the fir needles and put his hand to the left side of his face, howling. Martin had grappled with the other town boy and got him in a wrestling hold that left him almost unable to see or hear. Johnny untied the swollen-faced Kreuzkamm.

'Quick!' cried Martin. 'We must be back on the building site in two minutes' time!'

Rudi Kreuzkamm stretched. All his joints hurt. His cheeks were as thick as if he had a dumpling in his mouth. 'I've been sitting on that chair since one-thirty,' he said, kicking it. 'And now it's four o'clock. Not to mention six slaps every ten minutes!'

'That's no joke,' Matthias agreed, picking up the washing line. They stood the two town boys back to back and tied them up very thoroughly. 'There,' said Martin. 'Now, hurry up and pay them back those slaps! Two and a half hours are a hundred and fifty minutes. How many slaps does that come to, Kurt?'

'Ninety,' replied Kurt tearfully. 'Forty-five each.'

'There isn't time for that,' said Matthias. 'I'll give each of them one slap in the face. That'll be just as good as Rudi giving them ninety.' Here the other town boy began crying too.

'Where are the dictation exercise books, Rudi?' asked Martin.

Kreuzkamm pointed to a corner of the cellar.

'I can't see them,' said Martin.

'Look more closely,' replied Kreuzkamm.

There was a heap of ashes in the corner. A little charred paper and part of a blue exercise book cover could still be seen.

'Holy Moses!' said Matthias. 'Is that all that's left of our dictation exercise books?'

Kreuzkamm nodded. 'They burnt them before my eyes.'

'Won't your old man just be pleased!' said Martin. Then he took out his handkerchief, swept the ashes into it, tied its corners carefully together and put the remains of the exercise books in his pocket.

'This is a nice state of affairs!' said Johnny.

Matthias rubbed his hands with satisfaction. 'I'll donate an urn for the ashes,' he said, 'and we'll bury the dictation exercise books in No-Smoking's garden. Condolences declined with thanks.'

Martin thought, and then said, 'Rudi, you run straight home! If your father asks about the exercise books, tell him they're still at school and I'll give them to him in the first period tomorrow. Okay? Don't say anything else. We'll just give the town boys a quick thrashing on the building site and then we're off home. I bet handsome Theodor will be expecting us. Off we go!'

They left the cellar, except for Matthias, who stayed behind. As they were climbing the stairs they heard two loud slaps, one after the other. And then the sound of two boys howling their eyes out.

Matthias caught up with the other three in the yard. 'There, that ought to teach them a lesson,' he said. 'They won't be locking up any grammar school boys again in a hurry.'

Kreuzkamm said goodbye when they reached his door.

'And thanks a lot,' he added, shaking hands with them. 'All the best!'

'Same to you!' they replied, racing round the corner. Kreuzkamm cautiously felt his cheeks, shook his head and trotted off home.

Martin stopped them before they reached the building site. 'Johnny,' he said, 'you run in to our men and tell Sebastian it's all right for them to win now. Got that? So you all go on the attack at once, and as soon as it's hand-to-hand fighting Matthias and I will fall on them from the rear. Off you go!'

Johnny ran as if he were running for his life.

Matz and Martin peered through a crack in the fence round the building site. Sebastian and the others had let the town boys drive them into a corner. Snowballs were falling like hail. The town boys were chanting, 'Here we go, here we go!' as if they had already won the fight.

'Can you spot Uli?' asked Matthias.

'No, I can't see him,' said Martin. 'Watch out, Matz! Over the fence!' They climbed it and arrived at just the right moment. Sebastian was doing a good job. The grammar school boys, entirely unexpectedly, stormed forward. The town boys retreated from the attack.

Matthias and Martin ran across the site and hit the backs of the retreating enemy. Many of them fell in the snow and stayed there in their fright.

'Keep going!' That cry could be heard everywhere. Wherever Matz appeared, the enemy took to their heels. Some of them ran away separately, some ran away in whole troops.

Only Egerland stood his ground. He was bleeding; his expression was dark and determined. He looked like an unhappy king whose followers had deserted him. Little Barrel began running towards him.

But Martin got between him and the enemy leader, shouting, 'We'll give him free passage. He's the only one of them who behaved decently and bravely to the last.'

Egerland turned and left the battlefield, defeated and lonely.

Then Fridolin came over to the friends. 'Is Kreuzkamm free again?'

Martin nodded.

'How about your dictation exercise books?' asked Little Barrel, sounding keen to know.

'In my handkerchief,' said Martin, showing the remains to the respectfully admiring crowd.

'Who'd ever have thought it?' remarked Sebastian.

'Where's Uli?' asked Matthias.

Little Barrel jerked his thumb behind him. Matthias ran to the far corner of the site. Uli was sitting on a plank there, staring at the snow.

'What happened, littl'un?' asked Matthias.

'Nothing special,' said Uli quietly. 'I ran away again. Wawerka, of all people, came running at me. I was going to trip him up, honest I was, but when I saw his face I didn't.'

'You're right, he has a really horrible face,' said Matthias. 'I almost felt ill myself when he made for me.'

'You're trying to cheer me up, Matz,' said Uli. 'But I can't go on like this. Something has to be done about it, and soon.'

'Well, come along,' said Matthias. 'The others are leaving.'

And the two unlikely friends followed the rest of the boys. They all jogged back to school, and very likely straight into the clutches of handsome Theodor.

The defeated army from the school in town assembled in the yard of Number 17 Förstereistrasse. They were waiting for Egerland.

He arrived with a serious expression on his face, and said, 'Set the prisoner free!'

'We're not going to do any such thing,' cried Wawerka.

'Then do whatever you like,' said Egerland, 'but find yourselves another leader.' He went indoors without looking at any of them.

The rest of the town boys stormed down to the cellar, shouting. They were planning to take out their fury on the prisoner.

But instead of one prisoner they found two! All of them looked downcast, and they were finally feeling as ashamed of themselves as they could.

Chapter Five

The boys run into handsome Theodor again
· A discussion of the boarding house rules ·
Unexpected praise · A suitable punishment
· The housemaster's long story · And what
the boys said about it afterwards

It was late in the afternoon, just after five o'clock. The snow had stopped falling, but heavy, sulphur-yellow clouds hung in the sky. The winter evening was falling over the town; it was one of the last few evenings before the best one in the whole year, Christmas Eve. You couldn't look up at the many windows in all the many buildings without thinking that, in a few days' time, candles burning on Christmas trees would be shining down on the dark streets. And then you would be at home with your parents, under your family's own Christmas tree.

The brightly lit shops were decorated with evergreen branches and glass baubles. Grown-ups were going from one to another of them with packages, looking extremely mysterious.

There was a smell of gingerbread in the air, as if the streets were paved with it.

The five boys ran uphill, gasping for breath. 'I'm getting a punch-ball for Christmas,' said Matthias. 'I'm sure Justus will let me set it up in the gym. Wow, it'll be great!'

'The swelling on your eye is going down,' said Uli.

'It's nothing. All in the day's work for a boxer.'

They were getting close to the school. It was already in view, towering above the town. And with lights on in the upper storeys, it looked like a huge ocean-going steamer making its way across the sea by night. Right at the top, in the left-hand tower, two windows shone on their own. That was where Dr Johann Bökh the housemaster lived.

'Do we have any arithmetic to do for homework?' asked Johnny Trotz.

'Yes,' said Martin, 'practical exercises working out percentages, but they're easy-peasy. I'll do them after supper.'

'And I'll copy them from you tomorrow morning,' said Sebastian. 'It would be a shame to waste time. I'm just reading a book about the laws of heredity. That's much more interesting.'

The boys, out of breath, went on up the hill, with snow crunching beneath their feet.

S omeone was marching up and down outside the school gate, smoking a cigarette. It was handsome Theodor, no less. 'So there you are, my dear little kiddywinks,' he said nastily. 'Bunking off to the cinema on the sly, eh? I hope it was a good film—worth the punishment you'll get.'

'It was a terrific film,' said Sebastian, lying for all he was worth. 'The star looked amazingly like you, only not so pretty.'

Matthias laughed, but Martin said, 'Put a sock in it, okay?'

'And of course you're one of the missing party!' said handsome Theodor, acting as if he'd only just noticed Martin. 'Why

anyone would go handing out scholarships to someone like you I suppose I'll never understand.'

'Don't give up hope,' said Johnny. 'You're still young.'

Handsome Theodor looked as if he could have breathed fire and brimstone. 'Come along then, you lot. Dr Bökh can't wait to see you.'

They climbed the spiral staircase in the tower wing. The sixth-former marched along behind them like a policeman, as if he were afraid they might cut and run again.

A minute later they were all in Justus the housemaster's study. 'Here are the runaways, Dr Bökh,' said handsome Theodor. His voice was sugary-sweet.

Bökh sat at his desk looking at the five fourth-formers. His face gave none of his thoughts away. The boys' appearance told its own story. Matthias had a black eye. One knee of Sebastian's trousers was torn. Uli's face and hands were purple with the freezing cold. Martin's hair was hanging over his face, and Johnny's upper lip was bleeding. There had been a stone hidden in one of the snowballs that hit him. And the snow, dripping from five pairs of boots as it melted, formed five little puddles.

Dr Bökh got to his feet and went up to the guilty boys. 'What do the boarding house rules say about going into town, Uli?'

'The boarders are not allowed to leave the school building during break periods,' replied Uli, sounding scared.

'Are there any exceptions?' asked Bökh. 'Matthias?'

'Yes, sir,' said Matz. 'It's all right if a member of staff tells you or allows you to leave the school building.'

'And which member of staff told you to go into town?' asked the housemaster.

'None of them,' replied Johnny.

'Then who gave you permission?'

'We went off without permission,' explained Matthias.

'It wasn't like that,' said Martin. 'I told the others to follow me, that's what happened. I'm the only one responsible.'

'I'm well aware of your liking for taking responsibility, my dear Martin,' said Dr Bökh sternly. 'You shouldn't misuse that privilege.'

'He didn't misuse it,' cried Sebastian. 'We had to go into town. It was terribly urgent.'

'Then why didn't you come and ask my permission? It was up to me to give it or not.'

'You wouldn't have given permission because it was against the rules,' said Martin. 'And then we'd have had to run off to town all the same, and that would have been even worse!'

'You mean you'd have acted against my express prohibition?' asked Justus.

'Yes, we would!' replied all five.

'Unfortunately,' added Uli sheepishly.

'This is outrageous, Dr Bökh!' said handsome Theodor, shaking his head.

'I don't remember asking you for your opinion,' said Dr Bökh. And handsome Theodor went as red as a turkey. 'Why did you boys have to go into town?' asked the housemaster.

'It was the boys from the town school again,' Martin told him. 'They had attacked one of our day-boys. He'd disappeared, and so had the dictation exercise books that he was taking to Professor Kreuzkamm to be corrected. Another of the day-boys told us. So it was obvious that we had to go down into town to set the prisoner free.'

'Did you set him free?' asked the housemaster.

'Yes, we did!' cried four of them. Uli kept quiet. He didn't feel worthy to answer the question with a 'Yes!'

Dr Bökh looked at Johnny's split lip and Matthias's black eye. Then he asked, 'Was anyone hurt?'

'No idea,' said Matthias. 'Er... no one.'

'Only the dictation exercise books...' said Sebastian.

Martin looked at him so angrily that he stopped short.

'What happened to the exercise books?' asked Justus.

'They were burnt down in a cellar before the eyes of the prisoner, who was tied up,' said Martin. 'All we found were the ashes.'

'Martin collected the ashes in his handkerchief,' explained Matthias cheerfully, 'and I'm going to donate an urn for them.'

Almost imperceptibly Dr Bökh's face moved. For one-tenth of a second he smiled. Then he turned serious again. 'So now what?' he asked.

'First thing tomorrow I'm going to make a list,' said Martin. 'And I'll get everyone in our class to tell me what marks they got for dictation since the beginning of term. I'll write down all the marks and give the complete list to Professor Kreuzkamm when lessons start tomorrow. And we'll just have to do the last dictation again, the one that hadn't been corrected.'

'Oh, crikey!' whispered Matthias, giving himself a little shake.

'I don't know whether Professor Kreuzkamm will be happy with that,' said Justus. 'You probably won't all know those marks by heart. All the same, I must say that I approve of your behaviour. You did very well, boys.'

The five of them beamed like five little full moons. Handsome Theodor tried to smile, but it wasn't a very good attempt.

'However, leaving school without permission is still against the rules,' said Bökh. 'You look tired. Sit down on the sofa and we'll think what to do about it.'

The five boys sat on the sofa and looked confidently at Justus. The sixth-former stayed standing, although he felt like walking out. Dr Bökh paced up and down the room, and finally said, 'We could take the objective approach and just put it on record that you went out without permission. What's the usual penalty for that, Sebastian?'

'No leave to go out for two weeks,' replied Sebastian.

'Or then again, we could take the circumstances into account,' Justus went on. 'And if we do that, the first thing to be said is that of course, as reliable friends, you had to go down into town at all costs. What you did wrong was simply forgetting to ask permission.'

He went over to the window and looked out. With his face turned away, he said, 'So why didn't you ask me for permission? Do you trust me so little?' He turned round again. 'If so, I'm the one who deserves punishment. Because then I'd be to blame for what you did wrong!'

'Oh no, dear Justus!' cried Matthias, horrified, and then he quickly corrected himself, saying awkwardly, 'Oh no, dear Dr Bökh! I hope you know how much we all...' But he couldn't get it out. He was ashamed of admitting how much they loved the man by the window.

'Before we left,' said Martin, 'I did wonder for a minute whether we ought to ask you first. But I had a feeling that would be the wrong way round. Not because of trusting you, Dr Bökh. I don't really know just why I didn't do it.'

This was something else for clever-clogs Sebastian to explain.

'It's perfectly logical,' he pointed out. 'There were only two possibilities. Either you could say no to our request, and then we'd have had to go against your refusal. Or you could let us go, and then if anything had happened to anyone you'd have been responsible. And the other teachers and the parents would have gone on at you like anything!'

'Yes, something like that,' said Martin.

'You boys are positively addicted to taking responsibility!' replied the housemaster. 'So you didn't ask my permission just to spare me the awkwardness? Very well, you can have the punishment you're so keen to take. I forbid you to go out on the first free afternoon following the Christmas holidays. That will satisfy the boarding house rules, won't it?' Dr Bökh looked inquiringly at the sixth-former.

'Of course, sir,' handsome Theodor was quick to reply.

'And on that afternoon marked out for your punishment, the five of you are invited up here to the tower as my guests. We'll have coffee and a nice chat. That's not in the boarding house rules, but I don't think there can be any objection. Do you?' Once again he looked at the sixth-former.

'Certainly not, sir,' said handsome Theodor in dulcet tones. He felt like breaking apart into pieces.

'Do you agree to that punishment?' asked Bökh.

The boys nodded happily and dug one another in the ribs with their elbows.

'Great,' said Matthias. 'Will there be cake?'

'Let's hope so,' said Justus. 'And now, before I throw you out, I'd like to tell you a little story. Because I have a slight feeling that you still don't trust me quite as much as would be good for you, or as much as I'd like.'

71

Handsome Theodor turned and was about to tiptoe out of the study.

'No, no, you stay here!' said Bökh. Then he sat down at his desk, moving the chair so that he could look out through the window at the winter evening.

'The story happened about twenty years ago,' he said. 'At the time there were already boys like you in this boarding house. And stern sixth-formers like those you know today as well. And also a housemaster. He used the same study as the one where we're sitting now. Well, the story is about a fourth-form boy who slept on one of your iron bedsteads twenty years ago, and sat where you sit now in your classroom and the refectory. He was a good, hard-working boy, and he could get as vexed about injustice as Martin Thaler. He could also lash out like Matthias Selbmann when necessary. Sometimes at night he sat on the window sill in the dormitory feeling homesick like Uli von Simmern. He read terribly clever books, like Sebastian Frank. And he sometimes hid away in the grounds, like Johnny Trotz.'

The boys sat in silence on the sofa, side by side, listening attentively.

Dr Bökh went on, 'Then, one day, this boy's mother was very ill. She was brought from the little village where she lived to the hospital in Kirchberg, because otherwise she would have died. You know where the hospital is—the big, red-brick building on the other side of town. With the isolation ward in the grounds behind it.

'The boy was very upset. He didn't have an easy moment. And one day, because his mother was so ill, he just ran out of the school building, right across town to the hospital, where he sat by the sick woman's bedside and held her hot hands.

Then he told her he would come back the next day—because he had the afternoon free to go out that day—and he ran all the way back.

'A sixth-former was waiting for him at the school gate, one of those who aren't yet mature enough to make sensible and generous use of the powers they are granted. He asked the boy where he had been. The boy would have bitten his tongue off rather than say he'd been to see his sick mother. So, as a punishment, the sixth-former cancelled his permission to go out the next afternoon.

'But next day the boy ran away from the school building all the same. After all, his mother was expecting him. He sat beside her bed for an hour. She was even worse than the day before. And she asked him to come back again the following day. He promised he would, and ran back to school.

'The sixth-former had already reported to the housemaster that the boy had run off again, although he had been told he couldn't go out. The boy had to go up to see the housemaster in this very tower room. And on that occasion twenty years ago, he stood where you five were standing just now. The housemaster was a stern man. He too was one of those whom the boy ought to have been able to trust! But the boy said nothing. So he was told that he wouldn't be allowed to leave the school building for four whole weeks.

'Next day, however, he went off again. This time he was sent to see the headmaster of the grammar school when he came back. The headmaster punished him with two hours locked up in detention. But the next day, when the headmaster told the housemaster to unlock the detention room so that he could see the boy and tell him off, there was another boy in detention instead! He was the runaway's friend, and he had had himself locked up so that the other boy could go back to see his mother again.

'Yes,' said Dr Bökh, 'those two boys were good friends! They stuck together later, as well. When they had finished school they went to college to study together, and they lived close together. They didn't separate even when the first of the friends got married. But then his wife had a baby, and the baby died, and so did the baby's mother. And on the day after the funeral the husband had disappeared. And this friend, whose story I am telling you, never heard from him again.' Dr Bökh propped his head on his hand, looking very, very sad.

'At the time,' he went on at last, 'the headmaster was furious when he stood there in the detention room and realized that he had been tricked. Then the boy in the detention room told him why the other boy kept running away, and the story had a happy ending after all. But the boy whose mother had been in hospital decided that one day he himself would be housemaster in the school where he had suffered as a child because he couldn't entirely trust anyone. He'd do it so that the boys would have someone who was ready to hear all about their troubles.'

Justus stood up. The expression on his face was both friendly and serious. He looked at the five boys for a long time. 'And do you know what that boy's name was?'

'Yes,' said Martin quietly. 'His name was Johann Bökh.'

Justus nodded. 'Now then, off you go, you bandits!'

So they stood up, bowed solemnly and left the room. Handsome Theodor walked past them with his head bent.

Out on the stairs, Matthias said, 'I'd go to the gallows for that man if I had to!'

Uli looked as if he had been crying inside himself. 'Me too,' he said.

Before they went to their different living rooms, Johnny stopped in the corridor. 'And do all of you also know,' he asked, 'who the friend is who took detention for him, and disappeared without trace the day after the funeral of the baby and the baby's mother?'

'No idea,' said Matthias. 'How on earth would we know that?'

'But we do,' said Johnny Trotz. 'We all know him. He lives not far from here, and he jumped when he heard Bökh's name.'

'You're right,' said Martin. 'You must definitely be right, Johnny! We know his lost friend!'

'Oh, come on, out with it!' said Matthias impatiently.

And Johnny said, 'He's No-Smoking.'

Chapter Six

*A painting of a coach-and-six · An old joke goes
down well · Balduin as a first name · A damp
surprise · A ghostly procession · Itching powder
sprinkled by a weird apparition · Johnny on
the window sill and his plans for the future*

After supper they climbed the stairs to their study rooms
again. Martin did the arithmetic exercises for next day, and
drew up the list where he was going to enter their marks for
the earlier dictation tests that had been burnt along with the
latest, uncorrected one. Matthias, when asked what his marks
had been, couldn't remember. 'You'd better say I got a Four for
all the dictations,' he finally decided. 'I think I can get away
with that.' Then Matthias went to see the caretaker and borrow
a hammer and nails, and made a lot of noise nailing evergreen
branches to the walls—until the occupants of the other study
rooms sent urgent messages asking whether the boys in Room
9 had gone out of their tiny minds.

Handsome Theodor, as the senior prefect in Room 9, was
not his usual self at all. When Martin asked whether he could
go to the other study rooms to collect dictation marks from
any of his class who were working there, the sixth-former said,
'That's fine, Martin. But don't be gone too long.'

Matthias stared at Martin in astonishment. The others in the room, who couldn't know what had just gone on in the housemaster's study, sat there open-mouthed, and the other sixth-former present was so startled that he let his cigar go out. 'What's come over you, Theo?' he asked. 'Are you sickening for something?'

Martin was uncomfortable about all this, and he quickly left the room. When he had rounded up all the other fourth-formers who were boarders and entered their marks on the list, he ended up with Johnny Trotz. The prefect in Johnny's room was nice. 'Hello, Martin, on the warpath again?' he asked.

'No, not this time,' said Martin. 'Johnny and I want to discuss a Christmas surprise, that's all.' The two friends whispered together, and agreed to try to get Justus over to the allotments after lunch next day.

'Let's hope we're not wrong,' said Martin. 'It'll be a terrible mess if we are. Suppose No-Smoking and Justus suddenly say they never knew each other at all!'

'That's out of the question,' said Johnny firmly. 'I'm never wrong about things like this. You can take my word for it!' He thought for a moment. 'Don't forget, it can't be just a coincidence that No-Smoking and his railway carriage came to this town near our school! So yes, he wanted to live alone, and he moved from his old surroundings years ago without leaving any trace. But he couldn't tear himself away from the past entirely. And when he talks to us he's thinking about himself when he was a boy. I understand all that so well, Martin, it's as if I'd lived through it myself.'

'You're probably right,' said Martin. 'My word, won't they be pleased to see each other again!'

Johnny nodded enthusiastically. 'As soon as we see that we're right,' he added, 'we'll fade out of the picture as inconspicuously as possible.'

'You bet,' murmured Martin. Then he went back to Room 9 and took a picture he had painted for his parents out of his desk. It wasn't finished yet, and he went on working on it. He wanted to put it under the Christmas tree at home. Tomorrow, or the day after tomorrow at the latest, the money that his mother was sending for the fare would be sure to arrive.

The picture was rather strange. You could see a green lake in it, and high mountains covered with snow. Orange trees with large oranges growing on them stood on the banks of the lake, and there were palm trees as well. Gilded gondolas and boats with russet-red sails were passing over the lake, and a blue coach was driving along the road on the bank, drawn by six dapple-grey horses. Martin's parents sat in the coach in their Sunday best, and Martin himself was sitting on the driver's box. But he was an older Martin, with a handsome dark-blond moustache. People in brightly coloured southern clothes stood beside the coach, waving. Martin's parents, with friendly expressions on their faces, were nodding in all directions, and Martin himself lowered his driver's whip in response to the greetings.

The picture was called 'In Ten Years' Time'. By that, Martin probably meant that in ten years' time he'd be earning so much money that he would be able to take his mother and father on holiday to exotic countries far away.

Matthias looked at the picture, narrowing his eyes, and said, 'Wow, one of these days I bet you'll be one of those great artists like Titian or Rembrandt. I'm already looking forward to saying, "Oh yes, Martin Thaler was my form captain at school when we were boys. What a fellow he was! The things we got up to—they were really food for thought!"' But saying 'food for thought' reminded him that he was hungry again, and he immediately sat down at his desk. There was always something to eat inside it, and he had fixed photographs of all the international champion boxers inside the top of the desk with drawing pins.

Even handsome Theodor asked to see Martin's picture, and said it was a good example of his talent.

It turned into a nice evening. The younger boys put their heads together and told each other the wish-lists for Christmas presents they had sent home. And then Fritsche, who was in the Upper Fifth, began telling a story of what had happened in lessons that morning. After a while everyone in the room was listening.

'Every year Dr Grünkern, the Head, makes the same joke. It comes when he's teaching the Upper Fifth what the moon is made of. And it's been told for over twenty years. At the beginning of the lesson he says: "We're going to talk about the moon—so look at me!"'

'Why is that a joke?' asked Petermann, one of the younger boys. But the others laughed and shushed him, so he kept quiet.

Handsome Theodor said, 'Not a soul laughs at it in our class.'

At that moment Petermann laughed out loud. He had seen the joke.

'The penny dropped, did it?' asked Matthias.

Fritsche said, 'We did it very neatly. We knew the joke was due today, and we'd discussed it all in advance. When the Head brought out his famous joke, the back row of the class laughed. So of course he was pleased. Then he was about to go on. But then the second-from-back row laughed. So Grünkern was pleased again.

'But just as he was about to go on yet again, the third row from the back laughed. All he did was twist his face. Then the fourth row from the back laughed, and he turned yellowish-green. And at that moment the front row laughed. That finished him off. He saw it coming. "Don't you like the joke, gentlemen?" he said. So Mühlberg stood up and said, "It's not a bad joke, sir. But my father told me that when he was in the Upper Fifth here, the joke was already so old that it deserved to be pensioned off. How would it be if you thought up a new one?" So Grünkern said, after a long pause, "Maybe you're right." And then he marched out of the classroom in the middle of the lesson and left us alone. He looked as if he were going to his own funeral.'

Fritsche laughed, and a few of the others laughed as well. But most of them didn't really seem to agree with Fritsche. 'I don't know,' said one of them, 'but maybe you shouldn't have annoyed the old boy like that.'

'Why not?' asked Fritsche. 'It's a teacher's duty to be ready and able to change. Otherwise the students could lie in bed and learn their lessons from gramophone records. No, we need human beings to teach us, not canned knowledge on two legs! We need teachers who must develop if they want us to develop too.'

And then the door opened and Dr Grünkern, the headmaster, came into Room 9. All the boys jumped up from their chairs.

'Sit down and go on with your work,' said the Head. 'Is everything all right?'

'Yes, sir!' said handsome Theodor. 'Everything's all right, headmaster, sir.'

'Glad to hear it,' said the old man, nodding wearily, and he went into the next room.

'Hey, do you think he was listening at the door before he came in?' asked one of the third form curiously.

'It can't be helped if he was,' said Fritsche unmercifully. 'If he'd wanted to be a civil servant or something like that when he was young, then he shouldn't have decided to be a teacher.'

Matthias leaned over to his neighbour, a redhead from the youngest class. 'Do you know what Grünkern's first name is?' The younger boy didn't, so Matthias told him. 'Balduin, that's his name. Balduin Grünkern! He always signs his name with just B followed by a full stop. He's probably embarrassed about that first name of his!'

'Leave the old fellow alone!' said handsome Theodor. 'We need him as a contrast. If we didn't have him, we might not know how lucky we are to have Dr Bökh for our housemaster.'

The other sixth-former's eyes were popping out of his head. 'Theo,' he said, 'you might as well admit it—you've finally gone round the bend.'

After evening chapel they ran down the wide stairs to the room where they had their wardrobes, put their day clothes away and then ran upstairs again in their long nightshirts, first to the bathrooms, then to their dormitories.

The sixth-formers could stay up longer than anyone else. Only those in the Upper Sixth who were dormitory monitors had to stay up, making sure everyone washed thoroughly, brushed their teeth and then hurried into bed.

Going to bed was quite complicated. You had to sit up in bed and wrap the huge quilt round yourself, and only then, as if struck by lightning, could you drop back on the mattress, making the iron bedstead clank.

In Dormitory 2 there was an incident. Some joker had put a basin full of water under Matthias's bedclothes. And when Matthias, tired after the day's adventures, fell heavily into bed it was into that basin of cold water. Cursing and with his teeth chattering, he jumped out of bed and pulled out the basin from under his quilt. 'Who did that?' he shouted angrily. 'What a nasty trick! Come on, who was it? I'll murder him. I'll feed his body to the birds!'

The others laughed. Uli, feeling anxious, came along in his nightshirt carrying his pillow.

'You lily-livered bunch!' yelled Matthias.

'Get into bed,' someone shouted, 'or you'll catch your death of cold.'

'Quiet!' someone else said. 'Here comes Justus!'

Uli and Matthias jumped into their beds. When Dr Bökh came in all was quiet in the large room. The boys were lying in rows, like angels with their eyes closed. Justus went along the beds. 'Well, well,' he said out loud. 'There's something wrong here! When boys are as quiet as this there's certainly been trouble earlier. Come on, Martin, out with it!'

Martin opened his eyes and said, 'Nothing special, sir. Just a bit of a joke.'

'Nothing else?'

'No.'

Bökh went to the door. 'Goodnight, then, boys!'

'Goodnight, sir!' they all shouted. And then they really did lie quiet and peaceful in their beds. Matthias yawned as widely as a lion, stuffed Uli's pillow between himself and his wet sheet, and went to sleep at once. Soon after that, the others were asleep as well.

Only Uli was still lying awake. First, he missed his pillow. Second, he was wondering yet again how he could get to be brave. Then he heard the bugler in the barracks blowing the Last Post to let the soldiers coming back know that they must hurry. Uli thought of his parents, and his brothers and sisters, and being at home in three days' time—and he fell asleep, smiling.

An hour later the sleeping boys woke in alarm. An infernal noise was coming from Dormitory 1. Suddenly the door of Dormitory 2 swung open as if pushed by a ghostly hand. And the noise got worse and worse. A few of the youngest boys put their heads under the covers or held their hands over their ears.

Suddenly witches and ghosts dressed in white marched into the dark dormitory. Many of them held burning candles. Others were clashing saucepan lids together. Others again were bellowing like hungry cattle. Last of all came a weird apparition—a huge white monster, hauling boys' quilts off them and shaking a mysterious powder into their beds out of a big paper bag. A few of the smallest boys were crying with fear.

'Don't cry!' Uli told the little boy next to him. 'It's only the sixth-formers. They always have a procession like this a few days before Christmas. Just take care they don't sprinkle itching powder in your bed.'

'I'm so scared,' whispered the little boy, sobbing. 'What's that great big monster coming last?'

'Only three sixth-formers at once. They've sewn several sheets together and draped the sheets over them.'

'I'm still scared, all the same,' said the little boy.

'You get used to it,' Uli consoled him. 'I cried too, my first year here.'

'Did you really?'

'Yes, I did,' said Uli.

The ghostly fancy-dress procession disappeared through the other door of the dormitory. Slowly, things calmed down. Only the boys in the front row of beds were scratching themselves for some time, and muttering curses into their pillows. The itching powder was taking effect. But finally they, too, quietened down.

Matthias hadn't woken up at all. Once he had closed his eyes, you could have fired off cannon beside him and he would have slept through the noise.

At last all of them were asleep. All of them but one. That one was Johnny Trotz. He got out of bed and stole over to one of the large widows. Swinging himself up on the broad window sill, he drew his feet up, tucked them under his nightshirt and looked down at the town. There were still lights on in many of the windows, and the sky was full of white flakes circling fast above the town centre where the cinemas and bars and dance halls were. It was snowing again.

Johnny peered down at the town. He thought: there are people living under every rooftop there. And how many rooftops are there in a town? And how many towns and cities in our country? And how many countries on our planet? And how many stars in the universe? Good luck is divided up again and again. And so is bad luck... I'm sure I'll go and live in the country

one day. In a little house with a big garden. And I'll have five children, but I won't send them overseas to get rid of them. I won't be as horrible as my father was to me. And my wife will be kinder than my mother. I wonder where my mother is? I wonder whether she's still alive?

Maybe Martin will come and live in my house. He'll paint pictures, and I'll write books. It would be a funny thing, thought Jonathan Trotz, if life didn't turn out all right in the end.

Chapter Seven

A description of Professor Kreuzkamm · A hair-raising incident · The sentence that the boys have to write out five times · Uli's strange announcement in break · A walk with Dr Bökh · A meeting at the allotment · And a handshake beside the fence

J ust before lessons began in the morning, Martin came out of the classroom into the corridor. He was holding the list of marks for dictation, and before Professor Kreuzkamm, who taught them German, reached the classroom he wanted to give him the marks and tell him about yesterday's misfortunes. Rudi Kreuzkamm, the German teacher's son, had just told him that his father had no idea about it yet.

The corridor was empty, but voices from several classrooms came out into the corridor and filled it with muted buzzing and humming. The sound was like flies shut up somewhere.

Then the teachers came down from the first floor. They were in a cheerful mood, laughing out loud. Each of them went into one of the classrooms, and the buzzing and humming slowly died down. Professor Kreuzkamm was the last teacher to appear. He moved stiffly, as usual, as if he had swallowed a walking stick. Dr Bökh was beside him, saying something interesting, because the professor was listening attentively, and he looked even sterner than usual.

Professor Kreuzkamm was a strange man. The boys had always been slightly afraid of him. That was because he couldn't laugh. Or maybe it was just that he didn't want to laugh! Either of those things was possible. Anyway, his son Rudi had told the other boys that his father never moved a muscle of his face in a smile, not even at home.

They could have got used to that in time, but it was made more difficult by the fact that although he never laughed, he kept saying things that made the boys themselves laugh. In fact they couldn't help it.

A couple of weeks ago, for instance, when he was giving back the tests in class, he had asked Matthias, 'What mark did you get for your last test?'

'A Four,' Matthias had said.

'Really?' the professor had said, 'Well, it's a lot better this time.'

Matz was already perking up.

Then the professor had said, 'This time it's a *good* Four!'

On another day, the coats cupboard in the classroom had been left open. Kreuzkamm had called out, 'Shut that cupboard, will you, Fridolin? There's a terrible draught!' And whenever you couldn't help laughing, you felt really silly, because Professor Kreuzkamm himself looked sternly down at you from the teacher's lectern, making a face as if he had a stomach-ache. You never knew where you were with him, because his expression didn't give away what he was really thinking.

But you did learn a lot in his lessons. And that, after all, was worth something.

So now Martin had to confess to Professor Kreuzkamm that the dictation exercise books had been burnt. A class of younger boys stopped to say something to Justus, and Professor Kreuzkamm came stalking towards Martin on his own.

'Anything the matter?' he asked sternly.

'Well, yes, sir,' admitted Martin sheepishly. 'The boys from the school in town burned our dictation exercise books yesterday afternoon.'

The teacher stopped in his tracks. 'Er... did you and your friends ask them to do it?' he enquired sternly.

Yet again, Martin didn't know whether or not to laugh. Then he shook his head, quickly told the teacher the essential points of the story and handed him the list of marks. The professor opened the classroom door, propelling Martin in ahead of him, and they both entered the room.

W hile Martin was waiting outside the door, something hair-raising had happened.

Some of the day-boys, egged on by Georg Kunzendorf, had put Uli in the waste-paper basket, and then pulled the waste-paper basket up in the air by the two hooks used to hang maps in the classroom. Matthias, going to Uli's aid, had been held down on the bench where he was sitting by four boys. So now Uli was hanging just below the ceiling, red in the face as he looked out of the basket. Martin almost fell down in a faint.

Professor Kreuzkamm acted as if he hadn't noticed this scandalous state of affairs at all, but sat down calmly at the lectern, undid Martin's knotted handkerchief which was lying on the desk, and examined the ashes. 'What is this supposed to be?' he asked.

'Our dictation exercise books,' said Martin unhappily.

'Ah,' said the professor. 'I would hardly have recognized them. Who was given those exercise books at lunchtime yesterday?'

Rudi Kreuzkamm, the professor's son, stood up.

'Couldn't you have taken better care of them?'

'I'm afraid not,' said Rudi. 'Fridolin and I were attacked by about twenty boys. And before they burned the exercise books they'd tied me up with a washing line and locked me in a cellar.'

'How long were you in this cellar?' asked his father.

'Until about four in the afternoon.'

'Didn't your parents notice anything?'

'No,' said Rudi.

'Nice parents you seem to have,' remarked the professor with annoyance.

Some of the boys in the class laughed. It was funny, too, to hear the professor telling himself off.

'Didn't they wonder why you weren't home for lunch?' he asked.

'No,' said Rudi. 'Someone told them I'd been invited home by a school friend.'

'Give your father my regards,' said the professor sternly, 'and tell him from me to keep a better eye on you in future!'

By now the whole class was laughing. Except for Uli. And except for the teacher himself.

'I'll be sure to tell my father,' replied Rudi Kreuzkamm. That set them all off laughing again.

'A fine state you boys are in, I must say,' said the professor. 'And by the way, I don't need Martin's list. I have all the marks down in my own notebook. However, I'll compare the two lists. Let's hope no one has been improving on his marks. Well, we'll soon see about that. I would also like to let you know that the next time you get up to mischief I shall give you a dictation test guaranteed to take your breath away.'

They all stared up at Uli at the same time. This could be tricky!

'What, incidentally, is that waste-paper basket doing on the ceiling?' asked the professor. 'I do wish you'd stop playing such silly tricks!'

A couple of boys jumped up to haul the waste-paper basket down.

'No,' said the professor sternly. 'Leave it there for now! Plenty of time for that.' Could he really have failed to see that Uli was sitting inside the basket? 'Before we go on,' he said, 'let's just go over a few words from yesterday's dictation test. How do you spell *vertigo*? Sebastian?'

Sebastian Frank pushed his book about the laws of heredity under the bench and spelt the word. He got it right.

The professor nodded. 'And how do you spell *gramophone*? Uli?'

The entire class froze with shock.

The professor drummed his fingers impatiently on his desk. 'Well, come on, Simmern! How do you spell *gramophone*?'

A trembling voice inside the waste-paper basket said, 'G... r... a... m... o...' But Uli got no further.

As if drawn by magical attraction, the professor looked up at the ceiling, and he got to his feet. 'Since when has this classroom been a funfair? Will you kindly tell me what you are doing in that silly swingboat, Uli? Are you all out of your minds? Come down from there at once, boy!'

'I can't,' said Uli.

'Who did it?' asked the professor. 'Oh, all right. You're not going to tell me, are you? Matthias!'

Matz stood up.

'Why didn't you do anything to prevent it?'

'There were too many of them,' explained Uli, from up in the air.

'If there is mischief, not only are those doing the mischief to blame, so are those who do nothing to stop it,' the professor told the class. 'I want everyone to write that sentence out five times by the next lesson.'

'Fifty times?' asked Sebastian sarcastically.

'No, five times,' replied the professor. 'If you write out a sentence fifty times you end up forgetting it again. Only Sebastian Frank is to write it out fifty times. How does the sentence go, Martin?'

Martin said, 'If there is mischief, not only are those doing the mischief to blame, so are those who do nothing to stop it.'

'If only you knew how right you are,' said the professor, leaning back. 'That was Part One of the tragedy. Now get young Uli out of his swingboat!'

Matthias ran forward. Several other boys followed. And at last Uli had firm ground under his feet again.

'So now,' said the professor, 'comes Part Two of the tragedy.' And then he gave them a truly terrifying dictation test. It had foreign words in it, words in capital letters and words without any capital letters, difficult punctuation—it was enough to make you despair. The fourth-formers sweated blood over it for half an hour. In spite of the winter and the snow. (People were still talking about that dictation test years later. The best mark anyone got was a Three.)

'Oh, crikey!' Matthias whispered to his neighbours. 'Let's hope the boys from the school in town attack Rudi again today!'

But Professor Kreuzkamm took the dictation exercise books home himself. 'To be on the safe side,' he said, leaving the room with as much stiff solemnity as when he had entered it.

In break, Uli climbed up on the teacher's lectern and shouted, 'Quiet!' But everyone else went on making a noise.

'Quiet!' he called again. It sounded like a scream of torment, and now they did keep quiet. Uli was as white as a sheet. 'I want to tell you,' he said in a low voice, 'that I can't stand this any more. It's making me feel ill. You all think I'm a coward. Well, you wait and see. I want you to come to the sports field at three this afternoon. Three. Don't forget!' Then he climbed down again and went to sit at his desk.

'What's the idea, Uli?' asked Matthias. Martin and Johnny came up as well and wanted to know what he was planning.

He shook his head almost angrily and said, 'Just let me go, and you'll soon see.'

Before lunch the refectory prefect gave out the post. Matthias and a number of the others had been sent envelopes with money in them. It was the travel money they were expecting. Martin had a letter from his mother. He put it in his pocket. Although he had been at the boarding school for quite a long time, he still couldn't bring himself to read his post at the dining table, in the middle of the noise and with the boys sitting near him casting him curious glances. No, after the rehearsal of the play he was going to go out into the grounds, or into an empty piano room, and be alone when he opened his letter. He felt the envelope. It wasn't very thick. He thought that his mother was probably sending him a ten-mark note. The travelling money would come to eight marks, so he would have two marks left to buy a few little presents for his parents. The picture he had painted for them was very pretty, but he thought one picture wasn't much of a Christmas present for two parents.

When lunch was over, Matthias gathered his creditors around him and paid them back what they had lent him when he was suffering pangs of hunger. Then he ran off. He had to get to Mr Scherf the baker's shop. He was a rich man today, so he was going to buy cakes for all the actors in the play. Of course that included himself, because he was one of the actors too.

The refectory was almost empty. Only Martin and Johnny were still standing by the door. And at the back, by one of the narrow sides of the room, Justus was sitting at a small table lighting a cigar. They went over to him. He nodded in a friendly way, and looked inquiringly at them. 'You seem rather solemn,' he said. 'What's on your minds?'

'We wanted to ask you to go for a little walk with us,' said Martin. 'We have to show you something.'

'Oh,' he said. 'You *have* to, do you?'

They both nodded energetically. Dr Bökh stood up and left the refectory with them. He made no objection when they led him to the school gate. Then he said, 'Well, well. We go out here, do we?' They nodded again. 'I admit to being extremely curious,' he said. As they escorted him up the street, keeping close to the iron railings that made a fence round the school grounds, he asked how their rehearsals were going.

'We know our parts very well now,' said Johnny Trotz. 'Even Matthias won't let us down tomorrow evening at the

Christmas show. It's the dress rehearsal tomorrow afternoon. With costumes and all.'

Justus asked whether he was allowed to come to the dress rehearsal. They said of course he could. But he realized that they didn't feel entirely happy about that, so he said he would restrain his curiosity until the public performance.

'And where, I wonder, are you taking me now?' asked Dr Bökh. They did not reply but smiled. They were feeling very excited.

Suddenly Johnny asked, 'What was your friend's profession? I mean the friend you were telling us about yesterday evening.'

'He was a doctor,' said Dr Bökh. 'That's why he felt so particularly upset when he couldn't help his wife and their baby. He was a very good, efficient doctor, too, but sometimes no amount of knowledge can cancel out fate.'

Johnny had another question. 'Could he play the piano?'

Justus looked at the boys in surprise. 'Yes,' he said at last. 'He played the piano very well. But what makes you ask that?'

'Oh, I just wondered,' said Johnny. And Martin opened the gate to the allotment gardens.

'Are we going in here?' asked the housemaster. They nodded, and led him past a great many of the little gardens, all of them covered with snow.

'This was still all woodland twenty years ago,' said Dr Bökh. 'And when we boys had plans to do something here we climbed the fence.'

'We do just the same these days,' said Martin, and they all laughed.

Then the two boys stopped.

'Good heavens, I see that someone lives in a real railway carriage here!' cried Justus, surprised.

'That's right,' said Johnny. 'The man who lives in the carriage is a friend of ours, and we like him almost as much as we like you. So that's why we wanted you to meet him as well.'

Martin had gone ahead into the garden. He stopped at the railway carriage and knocked three times. The door opened, and No-Smoking came out. He shook hands with Martin, and then looked across the garden to the gateway, where Johnny Trotz was standing with Dr Bökh.

Suddenly Justus let out a deep sigh, flung the barred gate open and strode towards No-Smoking. 'Robert!' he cried, quite beside himself.

'Johann,' said No-Smoking, offering his hand to his friend.

It wasn't very difficult for the boys to steal away unnoticed, because the two men were standing in the snow like two stone statues, never taking their eyes off one another.

'My dear fellow!' said Justus. 'How very good it is to see you after all this time!'

Martin and Johnny hurried away past the gardens in silence. When they reached the fence on the side of the allotments nearest to their grammar school, they stopped to get their breath back. But before they climbed over the fence they shook hands with each other.

It was as if they were exchanging a silent promise. A promise that couldn't be put into words.

Chapter Eight

Contains a lot of cake · The next rehearsal of The Flying Classroom *· Why Uli brought an umbrella with him · Great excitement on the sports field and in the school building · Dr Bökh says comforting things · Martin reads his letter in Piano Room 3*

The last-but-one rehearsal of *The Flying Classroom* began with a great deal of cake. Matthias had splashed out generously with his money, and he made sure that none of the cake was left over.

Uli turned up late, carrying an umbrella under his arm. 'Why are you carting that brolly around?' asked Sebastian. But Uli didn't tell him, and no one asked any more questions.

He's changed a lot since first thing this morning, thought Sebastian. He's like a clock that's been overwound. Have *we* been winding him up too much?

Uli put the umbrella in a corner. He firmly refused to eat any cake, however much Matthias pressed him to help himself, and said it was time to begin the rehearsal.

So they rehearsed Johnny's Christmas play. They went right through it from Act One to Act Five without any hitches at all, and felt very pleased with themselves. 'There you are!' said Matthias proudly. 'The more I eat, the better I remember my words.' Then they discussed the costumes and props again. Fridolin was going to collect the blonde wig with the braided hair for Uli from Krüger the barber today, and bring it to school tomorrow morning. So there would be nothing in the way of the dress rehearsal. Even the Christmas tree had already been put up. It was covered with electric light bulbs, and the caretaker had put a lot of cotton wool on its branches to look like snow.

'Let's hope it all goes well tomorrow evening,' said Johnny. 'Mind you don't get stage fright. You have to act as if we were alone in the gym, the same as in the rehearsal just now.'

'Oh, it's going to be fine,' said Martin. 'But we must have a quick rehearsal for changing the scenery. Because if any of it falls over tomorrow evening, for instance the pyramid or the North Pole, the audience will be laughing before we've even opened our mouths, and if that happens we might as well not act the play at all.' Johnny agreed with him, so they got the large pieces of painted cardboard out of the corner again and quickly mounted them on the horizontal bars. Then they tested the plane to see if it could move from where it stood without letting the audience glimpse the boys hidden behind the cardboard pushing it along the bars.

'It all has to go smoothly,' insisted Martin. 'We must have the scenery up and running at a moment's notice!' They pushed everything back into the corner and then got it out again, handling it and cursing and swearing like experienced stagehands. Uli, unnoticed by the others, had stolen out of the gym. He was afraid they might prevent him from carrying out his plan, and he didn't want that.

Over fifty boys were standing on the snowy ice rink, full of curiosity as they waited for him. They were all from the junior classes. He hadn't told any of the older boys, but the younger ones had immediately felt sure that something unusual and forbidden was about to happen. They put their hands in their coat pockets and discussed what it might be. 'Maybe he won't even turn up,' said someone.

But here came Uli. He passed the watching boys without a word, and walked over to the iron climbing poles on the edge of the sports field. 'Why has he brought an umbrella?' someone asked. Everyone else said, 'Ssh!'

There was a tall ladder beside the climbing poles, one of the usual gymnastics ladders that you can find among the equipment in any school. Uli went up to the ladder and climbed its ice-cold rungs. On the last rung but one he stopped, turned round and looked down at the crowd of boys. He was swaying slightly as if he were a little dizzy. Then he pulled himself together and said out loud, 'It's like this. I'm going to put up my umbrella and do a parachute jump. Everyone step back so that I don't land on your heads!'

Some of the boys thought Uli was round the bend. But most of them moved back in silence, keen to see the exciting spectacle.

Uli's four friends, still at work in the gym, had finally pushed all the scenery and the bars on which it was mounted into the corner for today. Sebastian was grumbling about Professor Kreuzkamm making him write out the sentence explaining who was to blame for mischief fifty times. 'Fancy doing a thing like that the day before the Christmas festivities begin!' he said bitterly. 'That man has no heart.'

'Nor do you,' said Johnny.

At this point Matthias looked round inquiringly and asked, 'Where's young Uli? He's gone off somewhere.'

Johnny looked at the time. 'It's just after three,' he said. 'Wasn't Uli planning to do something at three o'clock?'

'Yes, he was,' cried Martin. 'On the sports field outside. I wonder what he's up to.'

They left the hall and hurried to the sports field. On turning the corner, they stopped dead. The field was full of students, all of them looking up at the tall ladder on which Uli was balancing with difficulty. He was holding the opened umbrella high above him.

'For heaven's sake!' whispered Martin. 'He's going to jump off that ladder!' He was already running over the sports field, now an ice rink, with the other three after him. In spite of the new snow covering the ice, the sports field was terribly slippery. Johnny fell over as he ran.

'Uli!' shouted Matthias. 'Don't do it!'

But at that very moment Uli jumped. His umbrella immediately turned inside out, and Uli fell to the icy, snow-covered surface of the sports field. He landed with a thud and lay still.

The crowd ran in all directions, screaming. The next moment the four friends were beside Uli, who lay there in the snow, unconscious and pale as death. Matthias was kneeling beside him and kept stroking him.

Then Johnny ran indoors to find the school nurse. And Martin hurried to the fence, scrambled over it and went to raise the alarm with No-Smoking. He was a doctor, after all, he'd be able to help. Justus was still there with him, too.

Matthias, who had stayed with Uli, shook his head. 'Oh, little 'un,' he said to his unconscious friend. 'And people are

always saying you're not brave!' Then the future international heavyweight boxing champion shed large, childish tears. Most of them fell into the snow. A few dripped on Uli's pale face.

Matthias, Martin, Johnny and Sebastian were standing in silence at the window of the anteroom to the school infirmary. They weren't allowed to go in. They didn't know how Uli was. No-Smoking and Justus, the school nurse and Dr Grünkern the headmaster were all inside the infirmary. The school medical consultant, old Dr Hartwig, had arrived as well.

Finally Martin said, 'It won't be anything too serious, Matz.'

'I'm sure it won't,' said Johnny.

'I felt his pulse, and it was perfectly normal,' Sebastian told everyone. This was the third time he had said so. 'I'm sure he's just broken his right leg.'

Then they fell silent again, and stared out of the window into the white grounds. But they weren't seeing anything; their gloomy thoughts cast a dark shadow. This waiting seemed to go on for ever!

Then the door opened quietly. Justus came out and walked quickly towards them. 'It's not too bad,' he said. 'The broken bone isn't too complicated. He also has bruising over his ribcage, but there's no concussion. So cheer up, boys!'

The four friends breathed a sigh of relief. Matthias pressed his face to the window pane. His shoulders were moving slightly. Justus looked as if he wanted to hug Matthias, even though he was so big for his age, but he didn't quite like to. 'Uli will be better in four weeks' time,' said the housemaster. 'And now I'm going to telephone his parents and explain to them why he'll have to stay here over Christmas.' He was about to go, but then he asked, 'Can any of you tell me why, for heaven's sake, he thought up that idiotic idea of jumping off the ladder with an umbrella?'

'Everyone was always going on at him,' said Matthias through his sobs. 'They said he was a coward, and stuff like that.' Matthias took out his handkerchief and blew his nose. 'And I was stupid enough to tell him, yesterday, that he ought to do something to impress other people.'

'Well, he's certainly done that,' said Justus. 'Now, pull yourselves together! Remember, breaking a leg isn't as bad as if your friend were to be afraid all his life that people would never take him seriously. I'm beginning to think that parachute jump wasn't such a stupid notion as I imagined at first.'

Then he hurried off to telephone Uli's parents with the news.

The four boys didn't leave until No-Smoking came out of the infirmary and assured them, on his word of honour, that Uli would be as good as new in a month's time. Matthias was the last to go out of the anteroom to the infirmary. He asked once again if he could go in and see Uli, but No-Smoking said that was strictly forbidden. They weren't to think of anything of the kind until tomorrow. So then Matthias went back to his living room in the boarding house.

As Martin went downstairs he felt his mother's letter crackling in his pocket.

He went into Piano Room 3, sat down on the window sill and opened the envelope. The first thing he saw was a set of postage stamps. He took them out and hastily counted them.

There were twenty stamps, each worth twenty-five pfennigs. Only five marks' worth in all!

His heart almost stood still. Then he picked up the sheet of notepaper. He turned it over. He put his fingers into the envelope. He looked on the floor in case there was anything else, but no. Only postage stamps to the value of five marks.

Martin felt weak at the knees. His legs were trembling. He looked at the letter and read:

My dear, good boy,

This is going to be a really sad letter. And I don't know how to begin it! Because this time, my dear Martin, I can't send you the eight marks for your fare home! We just don't have the money, and as you know, Father is out of work. When I think that you will have to stay at school over Christmas I feel terrible. I've thought of every way I could to avoid it. I went to see Aunt Emma too. But there was nothing to be done. Father went to see an old colleague of his, but he had nothing to spare either. Not a pfennig.

There's nothing for it, my dear, you will have to stay at the boarding house this time. And we won't see each other again until Easter. When I think of that—but we mustn't think of it, because thinking won't do any good.

Far from it, so we'll be tremendously brave and grit our teeth, all right? I could only scrape five marks together. I borrowed them from Mr Rockstroh the master tailor, until New Year's Eve. He wants the money back by then.

Dear Martin, please spend the money. Buy yourself a pot of hot chocolate in a café, and some cakes to go with it. And don't just sit about in the school and the boarding house, do you understand? Maybe you can find a toboggan run somewhere. You ought to get out of doors. Promise?

And tomorrow a package will come by post containing the presents you were going to get under the Christmas tree at home. Perhaps we won't have a tree at all this year. There's no point if you're not with us.

We can't send you much, but you know how short of money I am. It's very sad, but it can't be helped. My dear, good boy, we'll all be very brave at Christmas and not cry at all. Crying is strictly forbidden! I promise you I won't cry, and will you promise me the same, too?

With lots of love and kisses from your loving mother.

Father sends his love. He says you must be very good. But you're very good anyway, aren't you? I'm sending the money as stamps. You can easily get them exchanged.

Martin Thaler stared at the letter. The writing blurred before his eyes. His mother had cried over it. He could tell, because the ink had run in a few places.

The boy clutched the bolt over the window, looked up at the weary, grey December sky and whispered, 'Mother! Dear, kind Mother!'

And then he couldn't help crying, even though he was supposed not to.

Chapter Nine

*Sebastian makes statements of principle
about fear · A part in the play is recast · A
secret visit to the sickroom · The Last Bone
restaurant and a hot supper · Meeting a
postman · And Martin's letter home*

No one in the study rooms was talking of anything but Uli's parachute jump. And the whole school agreed: little Simmern was an amazing fellow, and the boys would never have thought him capable of such a daredevil plan.

Sebastian was the only one to disagree. 'That was nothing to do with being bold,' he said dismissively. 'When Uli jumped off the ladder he was no more courageous than before. It was despair that made him jump.'

'Ah, but the courage of despair came into it,' cried a boy from the Lower Sixth. 'There's a difference. A great many cowards would never in their wildest dreams think of jumping off ladders, however desperate they were.'

Sebastian nodded benevolently. 'Fair enough,' he agreed. 'But the difference between them and Uli isn't anything to do with courage.'

'What is it, then?'

'The difference is that Uli can feel more ashamed than they

do. You see, Uli is a totally simple, naive kind of boy. His lack of courage bothered him more than it bothered anyone else.' Sebastian thought for a little while. 'What I'm going to say isn't really any of your business. But have you ever stopped to wonder whether I, for instance, am brave? No, you've never noticed anything! So I'll tell you now, in confidence, that as it happens I'm unusually cowardly. However, I'm clever, so I don't let it show. I'm not all that bothered about my lack of courage. I'm not ashamed of it. I know that we all have our flaws and weaknesses. It's just a matter of not letting other people notice them.'

Of course not everyone understood what he was saying. The younger boys, in particular, didn't get it.

'I prefer it when people can still feel ashamed,' said the Lower Sixth boy.

'Me too,' replied Sebastian quietly. He was unusually talkative today. That was probably something to do with Uli's accident. In the normal way Sebastian only said sarcastic things that put the other boys off. He had no best friend, and they had always thought he didn't need one. But now they sensed that he suffered from his loneliness. He certainly wasn't a very happy person. 'And by the way,' he said, in what was suddenly a chilly tone, 'don't any of you dare make jokes about my lack of courage. Because if you do I'll have to hit you just for the sake of my reputation. I'm brave enough for that.' So that was it! Just now the others had almost been feeling sorry for him, and now there he went, putting them all off again.

'Quiet!' called the senior prefect in the room. He had been taking a little nap, and had suddenly woken up.

And Sebastian wrote out, fifty times, the sentence saying who was to blame for mischief.

A little later he went into Johnny's study room. 'Who's going to take Uli's part in the play tomorrow?' he asked.

That took Johnny totally by surprise. He hadn't even thought yet that Uli's accident endangered the performance of *The Flying Classroom*.

'It's not a very big part,' said Sebastian. 'We just have to find someone who can learn the words by tomorrow morning. What's more, the unfortunate understudy has to look like a blonde little girl.'

Finally they thought of little Stöcker, who was in the third form. Before asking him if he would help them out, they went to Living Room 9 to discuss it with Martin.

Living Room 9 was like a house in mourning. Matthias had been to see Justus and ask whether he could stay at school for the Christmas holidays. Because otherwise, he pointed out, Uli would be left all alone. However, Justus had said he most certainly wasn't going to allow any such thing. Matthias, he added, must be a good fellow and go home to his parents, who were looking forward so much to seeing him. Anyway, Johnny would be staying in the boarding house. And Uli's parents had said on the telephone that they were coming to Kirchberg on Christmas Eve to stay for a few days. So now Matthias was staring into space and feeling furious about having to go home for Christmas!

And a few desks away from him, Martin was sitting feeling very sad because he had to stay at school over Christmas. True, he had been telling himself for the last hour that Uli and Johnny would be there too. But that was different, because what would Johnny do if he went home to the captain's sister's house? There was nothing special about staying here if you had a father who was a bad person and, furthermore, was in America. As for Uli, his parents would be visiting him at school, and that was something at least. Besides, if you'd broken a leg of course you couldn't go away.

But I'm perfectly healthy, thought Martin. I haven't broken a leg, and all the same I can't go away. I love my parents very much, and they love me, and still we can't be together on Christmas Eve, and why not? Because of the money. And why don't we have any money? Is my father worse than other fathers? No, he isn't. Don't I work as well as other boys? Yes, I do. Are we bad people? No. So what's the matter, then? The matter is the injustice that so many people suffer. I know there are good people who want to change all that, but Christmas Eve is the day after tomorrow, and they won't be able to change things by then.

Martin was even wondering whether to go home on foot. It would take three days, in the middle of winter. The earliest he could get home would be the second day of Christmas. Would the five marks be enough for him to buy food and places to stay for the night? And then he'd have to come back to school after the holidays, and once again his parents wouldn't have any money for his fare!

It was no good. Whatever way he thought about it, he would have to stay here this Christmas...

When Johnny and Sebastian came into the room and asked if he thought that Stöcker of the third form would make a suitable understudy for Uli, he didn't even hear them. Johnny took hold of his shoulder and shook him out of his gloomy thoughts. Sebastian repeated the question.

Martin said, as if it didn't much interest him, 'Yes, I'm sure.'

The two others looked at him in surprise. 'What's the matter with you?' asked Sebastian. 'Is it because of Uli's accident? You mustn't worry about that. It could have turned out much, much worse.'

'Yes, I'm sure,' said Martin.

Johnny leaned down to him and whispered, 'Hey, is something wrong with you? Are you ill? Or is it something else?'

'Yes, I'm sure,' said Martin. Apparently he couldn't think of anything else to say. He lifted the lid of his desk and took some notepaper out of it.

So the other two went away again. 'What was all that about?' asked Johnny Trotz anxiously, when they were out in the corridor.

'No idea,' said Sebastian. 'Maybe he has a headache.'

Then they talked to the third-former Stöcker. He was very enthusiastic, although his enthusiasm died down a good deal when he heard that he would have to wear girls' clothes and a wig with blonde braids. But they said he couldn't let the senior boys down. Johnny handed him the manuscript of *The Flying Classroom* and Sebastian told him, 'You have to know the part by heart at midday tomorrow.'

So the younger boy sat down and set to work learning it.

Matthias hadn't been able to stand it any more, and had made an excuse to go out of the study room. Handsome Theodor, the senior prefect there, was still showing what an impression Dr Bökh's story had made on him yesterday, and was leniency itself. Now Matthias was lurking behind a pillar in the corridor near the infirmary, waiting.

He was in luck. After only a few minutes the school nurse came out of Uli's sickroom and went downstairs to get something from the kitchen. Matthias cautiously looked around.

A moment later he was standing beside Uli's bed. The boy was asleep. There was a smell of medicine. Matthias's heart was in his mouth. Deeply moved, he looked at his little friend's pale face.

Then Uli opened his eyes, and a tiny, tired smile appeared in them.

Matthias nodded. He couldn't speak.

'It didn't hurt too much,' said Uli. 'Really it didn't. And my parents are coming tomorrow.'

Matthias nodded again. Then he said, 'I wanted to stay here for the holidays, but Justus said I couldn't.'

'Thank you very much,' whispered Uli. 'But you go home. I'll be almost better again by the time you get back.'

'Of course,' said Matthias. 'And are you sure it doesn't hurt now?'

'Honest it doesn't!' whispered Uli. 'What are the others saying?'

'They're astonished,' Matthias told him. 'And they respect you enormously.'

'There, you see?' whispered Uli. 'You were absolutely right. Cowardice can be cured.'

'But little 'un, I didn't mean it like that,' said Matz. 'It could have turned out far worse. I'm not a scaredy-cat, really not, but you could offer me a million marks and I wouldn't have jumped off that ladder.'

Uli's face was bright with joy and pride. 'You wouldn't?'

'Definitely not,' said Matthias. 'I'd rather be called all sorts of nasty names.'

Uli was happy with himself and the world. In spite of the pain and having to stay in bed for several weeks. 'There's some chocolate on my bedside table,' he whispered. 'From the head-master himself. You have it.'

'No, thanks,' said Matthias. 'I'm not hungry.'

Uli almost laughed. 'Not hungry?' he whispered. 'But Matz! I order you to eat that chocolate, or I'll get upset. And No-Smoking said I wasn't to upset myself.'

So Matthias quickly took the chocolate bar. Uli went on looking stern until Matz had broken off a couple of pieces and put them in his mouth. Then he smiled happily.

At that moment the door opened and the nurse came into the room. 'You get out of here this minute!' she cried. 'Who'd have thought it possible? A great big lout like you, eating that poor sick little boy's chocolate!'

Matthias went bright red in the face. 'But he ordered me to,' he said, munching.

'Go away!' she said.

The two boys nodded to each other. 'Get well soon, Uli!' said Matthias, and he left the sickroom.

After evening chapel, Justus made a short speech to all the students. 'We must be heartily glad that the experiment young Uli felt he had to make was no worse than an accident, and didn't turn into a disaster,' he said. 'It could have been worse. For safety's sake, I would like to ask all of you present to take great care that courage of that kind does not, for instance, turn into a fashionable craze. I'm asking you all to make as little as possible of your courage or your lack of it. We must think of the school's reputation as if it were our own. Broken legs are evidence of courage that, in my position as your housemaster, I really do not want to see. I don't think much of them anyway. There we are, and now that's that. I'm going out for a beer this evening, and Henkel of the sixth form will represent me here. Behave yourselves, and remember that if you kick up a racket today I won't be able to go out in the evening again. And I think I deserve to give myself a glass of beer. So goodnight, everyone!'

'Goodnight, Dr Bökh!' they said.

D r Johann Bökh went down into the town. It was quite a long way; the Last Bone restaurant was out in the suburbs. No-Smoking had said that was where he played the piano.

'Music and dancing, no need to drink wine!' said a notice on the door. Justus went in. It wasn't a very smart restaurant, and the customers looked a bold bunch. No-Smoking was sitting at a piano that needed tuning, playing hit after hit.

Bökh sat down at a small table, ordered a glass of beer and lit himself a cigar. No-Smoking had seen him come in, and nodded to him. While his friend played, Justus looked all around. It really was a rough sort of place. When people went onto the dance floor, the men kept their hats on. The Last Bone was quite something!

About half an hour later No-Smoking came over to Bökh's table. 'This is the break period,' he said with a cheerful smile. The waiter brought him a plate of steak and fried potatoes and a small glass of beer. 'My hot supper,' explained No-Smoking, tucking in.

'Don't think I'm interfering, Robert,' said Justus, 'but this is no kind of job for you! Won't you try going back to your old professional life?' And when his friend didn't reply, Bökh said, 'At least try it, for my sake!'

No-Smoking shook his head. 'What's your idea, Johann?' he asked. 'I live very happily in my funny old railway carriage. The flowers will bloom again in spring, I don't need much money, and I've never had so much time to think and read before as in these last few years—although you think of them as lost years. But there was a point in my unhappiness of that time. There have to be eccentrics in the world, and that's what I've become. I never should have trained as a doctor, I should have trained as a gardener, but I'm afraid it's too late for that. And here, in this noisy, downmarket place, I feel as wonderfully alone as if I were sitting somewhere out in the forest.'

'Listen, Robert,' said Justus. 'Our school doctor, old Hartwig, is getting on in years. He has a large practice. I can't imagine that he would mind suggesting you as his successor as our school doctor. You'd earn as much in that post as playing the piano, and you could still live in your railway carriage. Well, what do you think of that idea? Shall I put it to old Hartwig?'

'Do, as far as I'm concerned!' replied No-Smoking. 'Ask him by all means, if you like. But my dear fellow, don't think it would make me any happier to be prescribing aspirins again one day. And don't tell me the usual stuff about people being unable to live without ambition. There aren't nearly enough who live as I do. Of course I don't mean everyone should play the piano in a shady dive, but I could wish more of us had time to remember what really matters. Money and status and fame are childish things! Toys, that's all. Those who are really grown-up can do without them. Am I right, my friend?' He paused for a moment. 'But of course, if I could make sure that all was well with the

115

health of your schoolboys—that wouldn't be at all unwelcome. I mean, I'd only have to climb over the fence if someone was ill. And I could go on growing flowers and reading books. So fine, old fellow, ask your school doctor! And if he shakes his head I can go on tinkling the ivories here. Anyway, I'm not giving up my allotment until Martin and Johnny, Matthias, Uli and Sebastian have taken their school-leaving exams.'

'And I'm not giving up my room in the tower until then, either,' said Justus. 'They're excellent lads!'

The two of them drank to one another.

'And here's to little Uli,' said No-Smoking as they clinked glasses. 'May he get better soon.' Then they told each other what they knew about the war between the grammar school boys and the boys from the school in town.

Justus smiled at his friend. 'Those lads like us both, if you ask me,' he said.

No-Smoking nodded cheerfully and said, 'Well, they're right, don't you agree?'

Then he had to go back to the out-of-tune piano, because the customers wanted to dance.

After midnight they went right through the whole town on their way home. They remembered many stories of their own young days. How long ago that was! But it had all happened here, in the same streets down which they were walking tonight. And what had become of the other boys who had sat at the same school desks as they did? They knew a little about some of them, but what about the others? The stars shone above them, the same stars as in the time of their youth.

The postman was just emptying the postbox on the corner of Nordstrasse.

'I wonder how often we used to run to that postbox?' said Justus.

'At least twice a week,' said No-Smoking thoughtfully. 'If I didn't write twice a week, my mother thought something had happened to me.'

As it happened, the postbox being emptied by the postman contained a letter to Mr and Mrs Thaler in Hermsdorf. On the back the sender's name was given as 'Martin Thaler, Grammar School, Kirchberg.'

'The postbox is the same,' said Justus, 'but it's a different postman now.'

The letter mentioned above ran like this:

Dear Mummy

At first it was quite a shock, you know, but after all there's nothing to be done about it. I didn't cry at all. Not a single tear. And I promise you and Father to buy myself cakes and hot chocolate at Mr Scherf the baker's. It's wonderfully cheap there, Matthias says. I'll go tobogganing as well if you like. Definitely. You can rely on me. And many, many thanks for the money. I'll take the stamps to the post office on Christmas Eve and exchange them there.

This is the first Christmas when we won't be seeing each other, and of course that's very sad, but you know me. If I make up my mind not to let anything get me down, then it doesn't. Why am I a man, after all? I'm looking forward so much to the parcel that's arriving tomorrow. I'll put some evergreen branches on my desk, and there are candles here, too. As well as me, Johnny is staying here for Christmas. You know why. And Uli, who has broken his right leg. That's much worse, don't you think? Johnny said it's not so bad here if we pull ourselves together, so there you are!

Dear Mummy, you know I can't give you and Father anything this year. Maybe next year I can give extra teaching to one of the new boys in the bottom form, and that will make me plenty of money. Isn't that a good idea?

But I've painted you a picture. It's called 'In Ten Years' Time', and you'll understand why. It shows me driving you over the Alps in a blue coach. I'm putting it in this letter, but I'll have to fold it twice, or it won't fit into the envelope. I hope you like it. I couldn't make it any better, but I spent two weeks painting it.

So now I must finish, dear Mummy, because the bell has rung for supper, and then I must just go down to the postbox.

Keep on loving me even if I can't get home for Christmas, and don't be sad. I'm not sad, honestly I'm not. You can rely on me. I'll go tobogganing and think of you all the time. I'm sure it will be fun.

Lots and lots and lots of love to you and Father.

From your son Martin.

The postman emptying the postbox had no idea how many sighs fell into his big bag. And nor did Dr Bökh and No-Smoking.

118

Chapter Ten

The last day of school before the holidays · A walk in Kirchberg and several meetings · Another bar of chocolate for Matthias · The Christmas celebrations in the gym · Someone unexpected in the audience · What he is given for Christmas and what he says · And a moment beside Martin's bed

The next day was the last day of lessons before the holidays. On 23 December, none of the students could be expected to show any interest in the nature of electricity, the infinitives of verbs, the calculation of interest or what the Holy Roman Emperor Henry IV did at Canossa. No teacher in the world can ask that!

And they don't. They certainly didn't at the Johann-Sigismund Grammar School in Kirchberg. Most of the boarders had already begun packing their cases. They were looking forward to the Christmas celebrations in the gym. They were looking forward to tomorrow's train journey. They were looking forward to the presents they would get at home, and to giving the presents they were taking home for their parents and brothers and sisters.

They were as pleased as Punch, as merry as a cricket, and they had to concentrate hard to keep themselves from climbing on the benches during the lesson and beginning to dance with glee.

All the teachers could do was make allowances for the mental instability of their students, and get them to read stories and legends aloud, or tell stories of their own if they could think of any.

In the last lesson of all, the fourth-formers had geography with Dr Bökh. He had brought a book of fables, and asked them in turn to read aloud some of those interesting short stories, almost all of them apparently about animals, and almost all of them really about human beings.

When Martin's turn came he stammered. He got words wrong. He skipped two lines without noticing. He read aloud as if he had learnt to read only yesterday. A few of the fourth-formers laughed. Johnny looked at his friend with concern.

'That was fine,' said Justus. 'I expect your thoughts are already under the Christmas tree at home in Hermsdorf. Just wait a little longer, and you'll be home with your parents soon enough!'

Martin bent his head and told himself: crying is strictly forbidden! Crying is strictly forbidden! Crying is strictly forbidden! He had been murmuring that to himself again and again yesterday evening when he couldn't get to sleep. He'd repeated it at least a hundred times.

Justus passed the book of fables to the next boy. He kept glancing surreptitiously at the form captain until the end of the lesson, and he seemed to be wondering what was going on.

Martin stared at the bench where he was sitting, and dared not look up.

At midday the postman brought the parcel that his mother had promised in her letter. The parcel of Christmas presents! Martin didn't even look inside it. He put it under his arm and took it to the room where the boys' wardrobes stood. Just as he had opened his own wardrobe and was about to put the parcel inside it, Matthias passed him, dragging a large suitcase. He was going to pack.

'Hello, who's sent you a parcel today?' he asked.

'It's from home,' said Martin.

'Why are they sending you a parcel the day before you see them?'

'My mother's sending my clean washing so that I won't have so much to carry on the way back in January.'

'Sounds like a good idea,' said Matthias. 'Well, I'd better pack my case. I'd rather stay here, but Justus won't let me. He thinks I ought to give my dear family the pleasure of seeing me under the Selbmanns' Christmas tree in Frankenstein. If he says so. Anyway, it's always fun to be home at Christmas time, don't you think? Isn't it the same for you?'

'Yes,' said Martin, 'Yes, it's a whole lot of fun.'

Matthias wasn't going to shut up. 'Are you going on the midday train too?'

'No, I'm going later.'

'On the 17:12?'

'Yes. The 17:12.'

'Oh, do go on the midday train!' begged Matthias. 'At least fifty boys are going our way at midday. We'll occupy a whole carriage and kick up a racket. It will be great! So will you come with us?'

Martin couldn't bear it any more. He slammed the door of his wardrobe, cried, 'No!' and ran out of the room.

Matthias shook his head, muttering, 'I wonder what's biting him?'

In the afternoon most of the boys went down into the town to do some quick shopping, or just to stand outside the toyshop windows. It had snowed in the morning, and now it was bitterly cold. The people selling Christmas trees on the street corners were trying to get rid of their last fir and pine trees, and were willing to haggle.

Martin went to the post office and asked the clerk behind the counter to exchange his postage stamps for money. The clerk growled like a lion, but in the end he brought out two two-mark coins and one one-mark coin. Martin thanked him politely, put the money in his pocket, and walked round the streets for a while.

In Wilhelmplatz he met Egerland, the former leader of the boys from the town school. They said hello like enemy generals on the Riviera after the war. Not as if they'd made up their quarrels, but respectfully.

And in Kaiserstrasse Martin met Sebastian Frank. Sebastian was looking awkward. He pointed to a couple of little packets he was holding. 'What can I do?' he said. 'It's the custom. Are you shopping too?'

'No,' said Martin.

'I always leave it till the last minute,' said Sebastian. 'Every time I think I won't do it. Because it's kind of an antediluvian custom, don't you think? But then I dash off all the same to get presents. And there's something in it. In the end I actually like giving the others something. It's nice, don't you think so?'

'Yes,' said Martin. 'In fact it's a wonderful custom.' Then he bit his lower lip. One more word and he'd have been in floods of tears. Crying is strictly forbidden, he thought, nodding to Sebastian and going on in a hurry. He was almost running. He wanted to get away, out of this Christmassy atmosphere! On the corner of Nordstrasse he stopped and inspected the window of Mr Scherf's bakery.

So this was where he was going to drink hot chocolate and eat cake. It would be awful. But it was what his mother wanted him to do, and he had promised he would.

Dear heavens, he thought, how am I going to last two weeks without once crying?

Then he trotted back to school. The two-mark pieces and the one-mark piece were jingling in his pocket.

The dress rehearsal of *The Flying Classroom* took place, of course, in costume. The boys had been afraid that little Stöcker wouldn't be any good, but they were pleasantly surprised. The third-former acted brilliantly! And wearing the barber Krüger's wig with its pinned-up braids, and Uli's costume as the little girl, he looked really good. Anyone who didn't know would have taken him for a real girl. 'The sixth-formers are going to fall desperately in love with you,' said Sebastian.

Only Matthias thought Uli had acted the part a little better, but that was understandable. He owed it to his friend to think so, after all.

They rehearsed the play twice. It was hardest for Matz. The short time he had to change his costume between Acts Four and Five was what really bothered him. Turning from being a polar bear to acting the part of St Peter within a minute wasn't easy. But it would be all right.

'That'll do,' said Johnny Trotz. 'Break a leg, everyone!' Sebastian had told them that was what actors always said before the show.

Johnny went over to Martin. 'What's the matter with you?' he asked. 'You know your part all right, but you're just going through it as if you were thinking of something else.'

'It'll be all right this evening,' said Martin. 'I slept badly last night.'

When they had changed again they put their costumes and the wig and beards in the cupboard where the springboards were kept. Then they went back to the school building and up to the infirmary. They had been given permission to visit Uli.

After they had asked how he was, they told him they were sure the performance would go well. Matthias said he thought that so far Stöcker from the third form was all right, but naturally he couldn't be compared with Uli. The others nodded.

'I'm glad,' said Uli. 'And tomorrow you'll all be going home except for Johnny and me. I hope you get nice presents.' Then he beckoned Matthias over to his bed and surreptitiously put a bar of chocolate in his hand. 'Dr Grünkern was here again,' he whispered. 'How's your appetite?'

'It's okay,' said Matz.

'You see?' said Uli. 'Keep on eating!'

'It's much worse for me at home,' said Matthias, putting the chocolate in his pocket. 'My old lady can't believe it. She says the amount I eat is positively criminal!'

'Think nothing of it,' said Sebastian. He was less impatient than usual today. 'A man must have what he needs.' Then he turned to Uli and shook his head in an avuncular way. 'You're really one of us now! It's lucky we don't have a church tower on the sports field, or you'd probably have hopped off that, too.'

They were standing round his bed, and although they said a lot they didn't really know what they ought to say. To them, the boy in the bed was no longer the same little Uli they'd known for years.

'It's a shame you can't be there this evening,' said Johnny. 'But I'll tell you just how it went down tomorrow.'

Martin was standing by the window. He really wanted to tell the others that he was going to stay here as well, but he couldn't bring himself to do it. In spite of his friends, he felt abandoned. Totally abandoned.

The Christmas festivities outdid all expectations. They began with two sixth-formers playing the piano. Variations on familiar Christmas carols. Then the headmaster, Dr B. Grünkern, made a short speech. It was like all the other Christmas speeches he had made in his life, but at the end he said a few things that were new, and touched the boys' hearts. 'I sometimes feel like Father Christmas in person,' he said. 'In spite of my black coat, and although I don't have a long white beard. I'm almost as old as he is. I come here every year. People smile at my appearance, but after all, he and I are both of us men who like children. Please never forget that. Because it excuses a great deal.'

He sat down again, and cleaned his glasses with his handkerchief. The youngest class bowed their heads, feeling ashamed of

themselves, because they had often laughed at the old man. And the tall Christmas tree was so bright with all its little electric lights that everyone present felt quite solemn.

Then came the performance of *The Flying Classroom.* You might as well know at once that it was a huge success. At the line 'Lessons on the spot itself' the teachers laughed as much as Sebastian had hoped. True, Martin was not at his best as an actor today, but the third-form boy Stöcker made up for that. He was very good, and apart from his own year and the fourth-formers, no one recognized him. They really thought he was a charming little girl, and they couldn't work out how a girl came to be here. Stöcker did get off his cloud rather too soon in the last act, but the Christmas carol that came next, with everyone singing in chorus, made up for it. The audience clapped and cheered.

With his coat-tails flying, the headmaster made for the actors and shook every one of them by the hand. When he came to Johnny Trotz he said, warmly, 'You're a real writer, my boy! How happy I am!' Johnny bowed. Martin's scenery won a lot of praise, too.

'And who are you, little girl?' the headmaster asked.

The whole audience listened for the answer—in particular the big sixth-form boys.

Then the little girl took off the blonde wig with the braids, and the next moment over two hundred boys were laughing loudly enough to make the walls of the gym shake. 'It's Stöcker!' they shouted.

They could hardly calm down.

Suddenly Sebastian said to his friends, 'Hey, did you see that? Who do you think is sitting there with the teachers? Right next to Justus? It's No-Smoking!'

Sebastian was right. No-Smoking, in his blue suit, was sitting among the teachers! Only Martin and Johnny knew how to account for that. And Johnny was already running out of the gym.

Dr Bökh got to his feet and went over to the middle of the hall. Everyone fell silent. 'A man whom most of you don't know is sitting on the chair next to mine over there,' said Justus. 'He is my closest friend. Twenty years ago the two of us were sitting side by side in this very gym. Not with the teachers, of course, but on the benches where you boys are sitting today. Several years ago I lost track of my friend, but yesterday, at last, I found him again! Two of you school students brought us together. I have never had a better Christmas present in my life. My friend's name is Robert Uthofft, and he is a doctor. Because I don't want us to lose sight of each other again in future, I had a word today with our good old Dr Hartwig.'

No-Smoking sat bolt upright.

And Justus went on, 'I asked Dr Hartwig to put in a word for us with the town council of Kirchberg, so that my friend Dr Uthofft could take over as doctor at our school here. And in future he and I, who met and made friends at this same school, will work together here again, he as your doctor and I as your teacher. The two of us belong to the school like the foundation stones of the building and the old trees out there in the snow-covered grounds. We belong here, we belong to you, and if you like us half as much as we like each other we'd be delighted. We don't ask for any more. Am I right, Robert?'

No-Smoking stood up, went over to Justus and was about to say a few suitable words. However, he couldn't get any of them out, so he simply pressed his friend's hand.

Then Johnny came racing in, carrying several small packages. He went over to No-Smoking, made a low bow, and said, 'Dear Mr No-Smoking or whatever your real name is, we didn't know that we were going to see you at our Christmas festivities this evening. Martin and Uli, Matthias and Sebastian had asked me to take these presents to your railway carriage tomorrow, when it's Christmas Eve. But now you officially belong with us, so I'd like to give you our presents today.'

And Johnny put the socks, the cigarettes, the tobacco and the pullover into Dr Uthofft's hands. 'If the pullover doesn't fit,' he added, 'don't worry, because the shop agreed to change it, and there's a receipt in the bag.'

No-Smoking put the presents under his arm. 'Thank you, Johnny,' he said, 'and many thanks to your four friends, who are my friends as well. The rest of you, those who don't know me yet, will soon get used to me. I'm not worried about that.' He looked all around him. Then he said, 'Dr Johann Bökh, known to you as Justus, and I have learned a few things here in this school, and outside it in life as well. And we haven't forgotten anything. We have kept our younger days alive in our memory, and that's what matters. You must forgive me for feeling rather moved. I hope you will understand. I even hope that you will feel a little moved yourselves. These things pass over. And I'm not much moved by cases of broken legs and pneumonia, as you will find out. Not that I'm inviting you to go and break your legs, most certainly not!'

No-Smoking linked arms with Justus. 'So not forgetting the main thing,' he said, 'I'll ask you at this moment, which I hope is a memorable one, not to forget your own youth! That may sound an unnecessary reminder now, while you are still children.

But it isn't unnecessary, believe us! We have grown older and yet we have stayed young. We two know what it's all about!'

Dr Bökh and Dr Uthofft looked at one another.

And the boys privately decided, in their hearts, never to forget that exchange of glances.

It was already late when Justus did the rounds of the dormitories, walking very quietly on tiptoe. The floorboards creaked quietly, and the little lights on the walls flickered with every step he took.

He stopped beside Martin's bed in Dormitory 2. What could be the matter with the boy? What had happened?

Martin Thaler was sleeping restlessly, tossing and turning in bed, and murmuring the same thing over and over again.

Dr Bökh bent down and listened hard.

What was the boy whispering in his sleep? It sounded like, 'Crying is strictly forbidden!'

Justus held his breath.

'Crying is strictly forbidden! Crying is strictly forbidden!' Again and again. Again and again.

He must be having a very odd dream—a dream in which crying was strictly forbidden.

Slowly and quietly, Dr Bökh left the dormitory.

Chapter Eleven

A railway station in cheerful uproar · A school without students · A disclosure in the bowling alley · A teacher who secretly climbs fences · A visit to Uli · Johnny claims that you can't choose your parents · And the same white lie is told for the second time

The morning of 24 December began with a crazy spectacle at the Johann-Sigismund Grammar School. The boys were racing up and down the stairs like lunatics. One had left his toothbrush in the bathroom by mistake. Another was hunting high and low for the keys to his case. A third had forgotten to pack his skates. A fourth was bringing in reinforcements, because his case was too full and wouldn't shut unless at least three boys were sitting on it.

The sixth-formers acted as if they weren't in nearly such a hurry. But when no one was looking, they raced up and down the corridors just like the smaller boys.

By ten in the morning the school was already half empty. The boys who were leaving later made enough noise for everyone, but experts could tell that the emigration had begun.

At midday the next troop left through the gate, which was wide open. The boys were wearing their caps tipped sideways

131

on their heads, and they dragged their heavy cases through the snow.

Matthias came stumbling along a couple of minutes after the others. He had been delayed by going to see Uli. Johnny, standing at the gate, shook hands as they said goodbye.

'Look after the little 'un!' said Matthias. 'I'll write to him often. Have a nice time.'

'Same to you,' said Johnny Trotz. 'I'll see to him. And now you'd better get a move on. Sebastian has gone ahead of you.'

'It's a tough life,' groaned Matthias. 'I have to drop in at Mr Scherf's bakery or I'll starve to death on the train, and I can't do a thing like that to my old folks. Listen, poetic genius, or whatever they call you, where's Martin Thaler? I wanted to say goodbye, but I can't find him anywhere. And it's difficult to say goodbye if he isn't around. Tell him Happy Christmas from me, and I'd like him to write me a card so I'll know what train he's catching on the way back to school.'

'That's all right; I'll tell him,' said Johnny. 'Now shut your mouth and get moving!'

Matthias heaved his case up on his left shoulder, crying, 'Hey, I'm getting a punch-ball for Christmas!' and went off like a trained railway porter.

The railway station was teeming with grammar school boys. Some were travelling north, others east. One of the two trains they were waiting for passed Kirchberg soon after the other.

The sixth-formers were walking along the platforms with the girls who were their dancing class partners, chatting like men of the world. They and the girls gave each other flowers and gingerbread. Handsome Theodor got a cigarette case that was almost real from his tango partner, one Miss Malvina Schneidig. He proudly showed it to the other sixth-formers, who went bright yellow with envy.

Sebastian, who was standing nearby with a crowd of younger boys round him, cracked jokes at the expense of the sixth-formers and won a lot of applause.

At last Matthias arrived. He sat on his case and ate eight pieces of cake. Then the first of the two trains came in. The boys going north stormed it like an enemy fortress. Then they looked out of the carriage windows and talked as loudly as they could to the boys waiting for the other train. A small boy from the lowest class held a notice out of the train. It said 'Password: Home'. Another little boy climbed out of the train again in tears. He had stupidly left his case on the platform. But he found it and was back on the train in time.

When the train left they all waved their caps. And the dancing class girls waved their tiny handkerchiefs. Some shouted, 'Happy Christmas!' Others yelled, 'Happy New Year!' And Sebastian shouted 'Happy Easter!' Then the train drew out of the station.

It was all very cheerful, and everyone was in a good mood except for the stationmaster. He heaved a sigh of relief only when the second train puffed out of the station, and there wasn't a schoolboy left in sight. From his point of view, that was as it should be.

T he school was almost deserted. You didn't notice the dozen or so boys who weren't leaving until the afternoon.

Then Justus put on his winter coat and went down into the quiet, white grounds. The garden paths were covered with snow. They were untouched; all the noise and laughter had gone. Johann Bökh stopped and listened to the sound of snow falling as the wind swept it off the branches. A time of peace and solitary reflection could begin.

When he turned down a side path, he saw footsteps in the snow. They had been left by a pair of boy's shoes. Who was walking around the school grounds on his own?

He followed the tracks. They led to the bowling alley. Justus tiptoed through the snow, along the narrow side of the wooden building, and looked cautiously round the corner. A boy was sitting on the wooden balustrade of the bowling alley. His head was leaning back against one of the wooden pillars, and he was staring up at the heavy snow clouds moving across the sky.

'Hello,' called Justus.

The boy gave a start and turned in alarm. It was Martin Thaler. He jumped down from the balustrade.

The housemaster came closer. 'What are you doing down here?'

'I wanted to be alone,' said the boy.

'Then forgive me for disturbing you,' said Justus. 'But it's a good thing I met you. Why did you read so badly yesterday morning, I wonder?'

'I was thinking of something else,' said Martin sadly.

'Do you think that's a good excuse? And why did you put on such a poor performance yesterday evening? What's more, why did you eat almost nothing in the refectory yesterday and today?'

'There was something else I had to think about, Dr Bökh,' said Martin, feeling terribly ashamed of himself.

'I see. What was it that you had to think about? Christmas?'

'Yes, Dr Bökh.'

'But you don't seem particularly happy about it!'

'No, not particularly, Dr Bökh.'

'When are you going home, then? On the afternoon train?'

And then two large tears ran down the fourth-form captain's face. Followed by another two. But he gritted his teeth, and no more tears fell. Finally he said, 'I'm not going home at all, Dr Bökh.'

'Well, well,' said Justus. 'You mean you're spending the holidays at school?'

Martin nodded, and wiped the four tears away with the back of his hand.

'Don't your parents want you to come home?'

'Yes, Dr Bökh, they do.'

'How about you? Don't you want to go home?'

'Yes, I want to as well, Dr Bökh.'

'Well, for heaven's sake!' cried Justus. 'What does all this mean? They want you to come home! You want to go home! But all the same you're staying here? Why is that?'

'I'd rather not say, Dr Bökh,' said Martin. 'May I go now?' He turned and was about to run away, but the housemaster held him back. 'Just a moment, my boy,' he said. Then he bent down to Martin and asked him, very quietly, as if not even the trees must hear him, 'Could it be that you don't have money for the fare?'

That finally put an end to Martin's brave attitude. He nodded. Then he put his head down on the snow-covered balustrade of the bowling alley and cried heart-rendingly. Grief took him by the scruff of the neck and shook him back and forth.

Horrified, Justus stood there waiting for a while. He knew that you mustn't begin comforting a grief-stricken person too soon. Then he got out his handkerchief, drew the boy towards him and mopped his face. 'There now,' he said, 'there now.' He was rather affected himself, and had to cough energetically a couple of times. Then he asked, 'What does the fare cost?'

'Eight marks.'

Justus took out his wallet and found a banknote in it. 'Here you are, twenty marks,' he said. 'That will cover the fare home and the journey back again.'

Martin stared at the banknote in astonishment. Then he shook his head. 'No, Dr Bökh, that's no good.'

Justus tucked the banknote in the pocket of Martin's jacket and said, 'Kindly do as I say, my boy.'

'But I still have five marks myself,' murmured Martin.

'Don't you want to give your parents anything for Christmas?'

'Yes, I'd love to. But...'

'There we are, then!' said the housemaster.

Martin struggled with himself. 'Thank you very, very much, Dr Bökh. But I don't know when my parents will be able to pay back the money. You see, my father doesn't have a job. At Easter I'm hoping to find a new boy who would like me to give him extra coaching. Can it wait until then?'

'Hold your tongue!' said Dr Bökh sternly. 'If I give you your fare on Christmas Eve, you certainly don't ever have to pay it back to me. A fine thing that would be!'

Martin Thaler stood beside his teacher not knowing what to do, or how to thank him. At last he hesitantly took the housemaster's hand and pressed it lightly.

'Now, off you go to pack your case!' said Justus. 'Give your parents my regards. Particularly your mother. I've met her.'

The boy nodded, and then he said, 'And please give your mother *my* regards.'

'I'm afraid I can't do that,' said Dr Bökh. 'My mother died six years ago.'

Martin made a movement almost as if he wanted to give his teacher a hug. But of course he didn't. He just respectfully stepped back and gave Justus a long, trusting look.

'Don't worry,' said Dr Bökh. 'You boys have given me your friend No-Smoking as a present. I'm going to celebrate Christmas with him this evening, over there in his railway carriage villa. And I'll have to see about Uli and his parents a bit, and Johnny Trotz too. So you see, I won't have much time to feel lonely.' Then he clapped Martin on the shoulder and said, with a friendly nod, 'I wish you a good journey, Martin.'

'And again, thank you very much,' said the boy quietly. Then he turned and ran away. Up to the school and into the room where his wardrobe stood.

As for Justus, he went on walking through the quiet, snowy school grounds. Until he reached the fence. Once there, he looked cautiously all round him, and then he climbed over it, just as he used to when he was a boy. He could still do it pretty well. 'Once learned, never forgotten,' he said to a freezing sparrow who was watching him inquisitively.

Then he went to visit No-Smoking, who had got a little fir tree. The two of them decorated it together with tinsel and gilded nuts.

When Martin was packing his case, Johnny came into the room. 'Oh, there you are!' he said. 'Matz wanted to say goodbye to you. You're to write to him at home and tell him which train you're catching back to school.'

'I will,' said Martin happily.

'Hey, you're beginning to sound normal again,' said Johnny, pleased. 'I thought you were going off your rocker. What was the matter?'

'Don't ask,' said Martin. (Because he couldn't very well tell Johnny, who had no home at all, why he had been so upset.) 'I can only tell you that Justus is about the best person in the world.'

'Do you think that's news?' asked Johnny.

As Martin was packing, he came upon his picture called 'The Hermit'. The one he had painted for No-Smoking. 'Goodness,' he said, 'there's not much point in that picture any more. Because he's not a hermit now, he's our school doctor. But maybe he'd still like it?'

'I'm sure he would,' said Johnny. 'It will be a souvenir of his last lonely year. I'll give it to him this evening.'

And then they went up to see Uli, who already had visitors. He was lying in bed smiling happily, with his parents sitting beside him.

'To think of the mischief he's been up to,' said Mr von Simmern.

'I don't think he'll do it again,' said Martin.

Uli's mother threw up her hands in horror. 'I should just about think not!' she said.

'There are some bad experiences that can't be avoided,' said

Johnny Trotz. 'If Uli hadn't broken his leg, he'd probably have caught some even worse illness.'

Uli's mother and father looked at Johnny blankly.

'Johnny is a poet,' Uli explained.

'Aha,' said Uli's father 'Well, of course that's something else.'

The two boys soon left. Uli promised Martin to get better again as soon as possible.

Johnny and Martin parted at the garden gate. Johnny could tell that there was something Martin wanted to know, although he didn't like to ask.

'It's a matter of habit,' said Johnny. 'It's not as if people could choose their parents. Sometimes, when I imagine them turning up here sometime to take me away, I realize how glad I am to be on my own. Anyway, the captain puts in at Hamburg on the third of January, and he's going to come and see me and take me to Berlin for two days. That will be great.'

He nodded to Martin. 'Don't worry. I'm not very happy, it would be a lie to say I was. But then again, I'm not very unhappy either.'

They shook hands. 'What's in that package?' asked Johnny. Because Martin hadn't managed to fit his Christmas parcel into his case.

'Clean washing,' said Martin, the same answer as he had given Matthias the day before. He could hardly tell Johnny that he was taking his own Christmas presents home! Or that he was bringing them back from Kirchberg instead of finding them under the Christmas tree at home in Hermsdorf!

Down in the town he bought a box of cigars for his father. Twenty-five of them, with a band round the middle of each, and a leaf of Havana tobacco laid over the top of them inside the box. And in a shop selling woollen goods he bought his mother a pair of warm, knitted slippers, because her old camel-hair slippers had been ready for the dustbin long ago, but she always kept saying, 'They'll last another ten years yet.' Then, weighed down by everything he had to carry, he went to the station.

At the ticket office window he said, 'A third-class ticket to Hermsdorf, please.'

The clerk gave him the ticket. He gave him some change, as well.

Martin put it all carefully in his pocket. Then he said, 'Thank you very much, sir,' to the ticket office clerk, and gave the man a beaming smile.

'Why are you so cheerful, then?' asked the clerk.

'Because it's Christmas,' the boy replied.

Chapter Twelve

A lot of beautiful Christmas trees and one small fir · Oranges weighing four pounds each · Many tears · A doorbell rings · Laughter and tears at the same time · New crayons and their first use · The Hermsdorf overnight postbox · And a shooting star

It was nearly eight o'clock on Christmas Eve. The official weather forecast was for heavy snowfalls all over Central Europe. And now the sky was proving that the official weather forecast was very well informed, because it was indeed snowing in the whole of Central Europe.

Which meant that it was snowing in Hermsdorf. Mr Hermann Thaler was standing at the living room window. The room was dark, because artificial light costs money, and the Thalers had to scrimp and save.

'I haven't seen such heavy snow as this for years,' he said.

Mrs Thaler was sitting on the sofa. She just nodded, and her husband wasn't expecting any answer. He was talking only to keep it from being too quiet in their apartment.

'The Neumanns are already giving their presents,' he said. 'Oh, and the Mildes are just lighting the candles! They have a lovely big tree. Ah, well, he's earning better again now.'

Mr Thaler looked down the street. The number of windows showing bright light grew by the minute, and the snowflakes whirled through the air like butterflies.

Mrs Thaler moved. The old, soft sofa creaked. 'I wonder what he's doing now?' she said. 'In that huge school building. It must feel strange when it's so empty.'

Her husband secretly sighed. 'You're making things too hard for yourself,' he said. 'First, Jonathan Trotz is there. He seems to like Jonathan. And then there's that aristocratic little boy who broke his leg, the one with *von* in his surname. I'm sure they're both sitting by his bedside, having a wonderful time.'

'You don't believe that yourself,' said his wife. 'You know as well as I do that our son isn't having a wonderful time at this moment. He's probably crept away into a corner somewhere to cry his eyes out.'

'I'm sure he hasn't,' Mr Thaler replied. 'He promised not to cry, and a boy like that keeps his promises.' Mr Thaler wasn't quite so sure of it as he made out. But what else was he to say?

'Promised! Promised!' said Martin's mother. 'I promised him not to cry myself, but all the same I was crying even while I wrote to him.'

Mr Thaler turned his back to the window. The bright lights on their neighbours' Christmas trees were getting on his nerves. He looked at the darkness in their own living room and said, 'Come along, let's have some light.'

His wife rose and lit the lamp. Her eyes were red-rimmed with crying.

A very, very small fir tree stood on the round table. Mrs Riedel, a widow who sold Christmas trees in the market place at this time of year, had given it to them. 'For your boy Martin,' she had said. So now the Thalers had a Christmas tree—but their boy Martin wasn't at home.

Mr Thaler went into the kitchen, searched around for a long time, and finally came back with a little box. 'Here are last year's candles,' he said. 'We burned them only halfway down.' Then he wedged twelve halves of Christmas tree candles among the branches of the little fir. It looked really pretty at last, but that only made Martin's parents sadder than ever.

They sat side by side on the sofa, and Mrs Thaler read Martin's letter aloud for the fifth time. She stopped at certain places and passed her hand over her eyes. When she had finished reading the letter, her husband took out his handkerchief and blew his nose hard. 'To think that Fate lets such things happen,' he said. 'A little fellow like our Martin has to find out how bad life is when you don't have any money. I hope he doesn't bear his parents a grudge for being so incompetent and poor.'

'Don't talk such nonsense!' said his wife. 'How can you think such a thing? Martin may still be a child, but he knows very well that being competent and being rich are very different things.'

Then she fetched the picture of the blue coach drawn by six horses from her sewing table, and carefully put it under the little Christmas tree.

'I don't know anything about art,' said Martin's father, 'but I really like that picture. Maybe Martin will be a famous painter some day! Then we really could travel to Italy with him. Or would Spain be better?'

'Just so long as he stays healthy,' said Martin's mother.

'And look at the moustache he's painted underneath his nose!'

Martin's parents exchanged melancholy smiles.

'I'm glad he didn't paint us in some showy motor car,' said his mother. 'The blue coach drawn by six horses is much more poetic.'

'And look at those oranges!' said his father. 'Oranges are never really that size. They must weigh at least four pounds each!'

'See how cleverly he cracks his whip, too,' said Martin's mother. Then they fell silent again, still looking at the picture called 'In Ten Years' Time,' and thinking of the little painter.

Martin's father coughed. 'In ten years' time! Well, a lot can happen by then.' He took some matches out of his pocket, lit the twelve candles, and put out the lamp. There was still a Christmassy glow in the Thalers' living room.

'You're a good, faithful woman,' said Martin's father to his wife. 'We can't afford presents for ourselves this Christmas, but we can give each other plenty of good wishes.' He kissed her on the cheek. 'Happy Christmas!'

'Happy Christmas!' she too said. Then she burst into tears, and it sounded as if she would never be able to stop crying again.

Who knows how long they would have sat on the soft old sofa like that? The candles were burning down and down. Someone was singing 'Silent night, holy night' in the next-door apartment. And snowflakes were still whirling through the air outside the window.

Suddenly the doorbell rang!

Neither of them moved. They didn't want their unhappiness to be disturbed.

But then it rang again, loudly and impatiently.

Mrs Thaler stood up and went slowly into the corridor. People wouldn't leave you in peace even on Christmas Eve!

She opened the front door, and stood there for a few seconds as if frozen rigid. Then she cried, 'Martin!' The name echoed through the stairway outside.

Martin? What did she mean? Martin's father started with surprise. He went out into the corridor, and couldn't believe his eyes!

His wife had dropped to her knees in the doorway and was hugging Martin, with both her arms around him.

Then even Mr Thaler's eyes risked shedding a tear each. He secretly wiped the two tears away, picked up the case lying forgotten on the floor and said, 'My boy, for heaven's sake, how did you get here?'

It was quite a long time before they all found their way back into the living room. Martin and his mother were laughing and crying both at once, and his father stammered at least ten times, 'Well, what a surprise!' Then he hurried back to the front door, because in all the excitement of course they had forgotten to close it.

The first thing Martin managed to say was, 'And I have the money for the return fare too.'

At last the three of them had calmed down enough for Martin to tell his parents how he came to be here instead of in Kirchberg. 'I really did pull myself together,' he told them, 'and I didn't cry. At least, I did cry, but by then it was too late anyway. Dr Bökh, our housemaster, noticed that something was wrong all the same. And then he gave me twenty marks. Down in the grounds, near the bowling alley. It was a present, and I'm to wish you a happy Christmas.'

'Happy Christmas to you too, Dr Bökh!' said Martin's parents in chorus.

'And I was even able to buy some presents,' said Martin proudly. Then he gave his father the cigars with the band round them and the leaf of Havana tobacco on top. And he handed his mother the knitted slippers. They were very, very pleased. 'And did you like our presents?' his mother asked.

'I haven't looked at them yet,' Martin admitted. So now he opened the parcel that they had sent to Kirchberg for him. He found some splendid things in it: a new nightshirt that his mother had made him herself; two pairs of woollen socks; a packet of gingerbread with chocolate icing; an exciting book about the South Seas; a drawing block and, nicest of all, a box of the best coloured pencils.

Martin was delighted, and kissed both his parents.

All things considered, it was the best imaginable Christmas Eve. The candles on the tiny Christmas tree soon burned down, but then they lit the lamp. Martin's mother made coffee. His father smoked one of the Christmas cigars. Then they ate the gingerbread, and they felt happier than all the billionaires in the world put together, living and dead. Martin's mother had to try on her new slippers, and she said she had never in her life had such a wonderful pair of slippers before.

Later, Martin took a plain postcard that he had bought at the station out of his pocket, and began drawing on it. With his new coloured pencils, of course.

His parents looked at each other, smiling, and then they looked at him. He drew a young man with two large angels' wings growing out of the back of his jacket. This strange man was flying down from the clouds. And below him, on the ground, stood a little boy with huge tears falling from his eyes. The man with the wings had a thick wallet in his hands and was holding it out to the boy.

Martin leaned back, narrowed his eyes in an expert way, thought for a while, and then drew some more things on the postcard: mainly a great many snowflakes, and in the background a railway train with a decorated Christmas tree growing out of the engine of the locomotive. The stationmaster was standing beside the train, raising his arm in the signal for the train to leave. Under the picture, Martin wrote in capital letters, 'A Christmas Angel Called Dr Bökh.'

His parents wrote a few lines on the back of the postcard.

'Dear Dr Bökh,' wrote Mrs Thaler. 'Our son is quite right to call you an angel. I can't draw, I can only thank you in words. Many, many thanks for the live Christmas present you have given us. You are a good man, and you deserve for all your students to grow up to be good men! With best wishes from your ever-grateful Margarete Thaler.'

Martin's father growled, 'You haven't left any room for me.' And sure enough, he couldn't fit in much more than his name. Finally Martin wrote the address.

Then they put on their coats and went to the station together, to post the card in the overnight postbox, so that Justus would get it first thing in the morning on Christmas Day. Then they walked home again, with the boy between them, arm in arm with both his parents.

It was a wonderful walk. The sky was glittering like a never-ending jeweller's shop. It had stopped snowing, and Christmas tree lights were shining in the windows of all the buildings.

Martin stopped, and pointed to the sky. 'The starlight that we see now,' he said, 'is many, many thousands of years old. It takes the rays of light all that time to reach our eyes. Maybe most of these stars died out even before the birth of Christ. But their light is still travelling. So for us they still shine, although in reality they have been cold and dead for ages.'

'Goodness me,' said his father. His mother was astonished too. They walked on with the snow squeaking under the soles of their feet. Martin held his mother's arm and his father's arm close. He was happy.

When they were standing outside their apartment building, and his father unlocked its front door, Martin looked up at the sky once more. And at that very moment a shooting star came away from the darkness of the night, gliding silently across the sky and down to the horizon.

You can make a wish if you see a shooting star, thought the boy. And as he followed the flight of the shooting star with his eyes, he thought: then I wish my mother and father, Justus and No-Smoking, Johnny and Matz and Uli and Sebastian too, lots and lots of happiness in their lives. And I wish the same for myself.

That was rather a long wish, but all the same he had good reason to hope that it would come true. Because all the time the shooting star was falling, Martin hadn't said a word.

And as everyone knows, that's what matters when you wish on a shooting star.

Afterword

*Buses and trams · Sad memories of Gottfried
the peacock butterfly and the calf Eduard ·
A meeting with Johnny Trotz and his friend
the captain · Greetings to Justus and No-
Smoking · And the end of the book*

Well, now I've told you my Christmas story. Do you remember that when I began to write it I was sitting in a large meadow? On a wooden bench, at a small and wobbly table? And when I felt too hot, I looked up at the Riffelwände mountains and the snow-covered clefts of the Zugspitze? Time passes as fast as if we were flying away from it.

As I write this Afterword I am back in Berlin. I have a little apartment here, up four flights of steps in a building with its own garden. My mother is staying with me at the moment, and she wants me to be home in good time. She is making macaroni with ham today, and that's one of my favourite dishes.

Just now, as it happens, I'm sitting outside a café on the Kurfürstendamm, the most famous street in Berlin. It is autumn. When the wind blows, yellow and brown leaves fall on the paved road.

What has become of that brightly coloured butterfly, Gottfried, who came to see me almost every afternoon for five whole weeks? Where has he flown? Butterflies don't live to a great age. Gottfried must be dead by now. He was such a friendly butterfly, and very fond of me. May he rest in peace!

And I wonder about the pretty brown calf who came to fetch me every evening in the big meadow, and took me back to the hotel down by the lake. What has become of him? Is he a fully grown bullock now, or was he made into veal schnitzels while he was still a calf? I liked Eduard so much. If he were to come trotting down the Kurfürstendamm now, give me that trusting look of his eyes and nudge me with his little horns—I'd shout out loud with joy. I am sure I'd take him in. Perhaps he could live on my balcony. I'd feed him on old seagrass mattresses, and in the evening I'd go for walks in the Grunewald forest with him.

But I don't see any calves passing by as I sit here. At most, maybe a few sheep, or a rhinoceros.

And the trams ring their bells. The buses drive noisily on. The cars hoot their horns as if they were being roasted on the spit. They are all in a tremendous hurry. Well, there it is, I'm back in the big city.

The wild flowers smelled so sweet at the foot of the Zugspitze mountain. Here, it smells of car tyres and petrol. However, I like them all: evergreen trees or factory chimneys, tower blocks or mountains with eternal snow on their peaks, fields of grain or underground railway stations, Indian summers or telephone wires, crowded cinemas or the green lakes in the mountains, city or country. Yes, I like them all. What would one be without the other?

Before I end this story, I must tell you about an encounter I had just now. Among all the people passing by, there was an officer in the merchant navy. A gentleman getting on in years, wearing a handsome blue uniform trimmed with gold lace and gold stars. And a boy in a grammar school cap was walking beside him. There couldn't be any mistake. They were Jonathan Trotz and his sea captain.

'Johnny!' I called.

The boy turned round. The captain stood still. I went over to the two of them and bowed to the captain. 'I believe you are Johnny Trotz from the Johann-Sigismund Grammar School in Kirchberg,' I told the boy.

'That's right,' he said.

'I'm glad to hear it,' I replied. Then I turned to the gentleman in the naval uniform. 'And you must be the captain who looks after Johnny like a father?' I asked.

He nodded politely, and we shook hands.

'You see,' I said to Johnny, 'I've written a book about you all. And the curious experiences you had at Christmas two years ago. I see you'll soon be in the sixth form, Johnny, so I suppose I shouldn't speak as if I knew all about you, but I don't think you'll mind. Do you remember how the boys from the school in town burned your dictation exercise books in Egerland's cellar?'

'I remember that,' said Johnny. 'You mean you wrote about it?'

I nodded. 'And about Uli's accident when he did a parachute jump.'

'You know about that as well?' he asked in astonishment.

'I certainly do,' I said. 'I know that and a great deal more. How are you all? Does Matthias still eat so heartily?'

'He doesn't exactly eat,' said Johnny, 'it's more like filling himself up with fuel. And he goes to a sports centre twice a week for boxing sessions.'

'That's great! How about Sebastian?'

'At the moment he's deep in his studies of chemistry. He reads terribly difficult books about electronic theory, and the kinetic theory of gas, and quantum mechanics and stuff like that.'

'And what about your special friend?'

'Martin is still top of the class. And he still gets furious over any kind of injustice. In his spare time he paints, but I expect you know that too. His pictures are very beautiful. A professor from the Academy of Art wrote to him and said he ought to become a painter when he grows up. And Martin's father has found a job again.'

'I'm really glad to hear that,' I said. 'How about Uli?'

'Uli's a strange person,' said Johnny. 'He's still the smallest in the class, but he's quite different from the way he used to be. Matthias does anything he says. And so do all of us, more or less. Uli isn't physically large, but there's a kind of power in him, and no one can resist it. Uli doesn't do it on purpose, but when he looks at you, you do what he wants.'

'He overcame himself two years ago,' said the captain thoughtfully. 'And once you've done that, nothing else is any big deal.'

'I'm sure that's the secret,' I said, and then I turned back to Johnny. 'Are you still writing?'

The captain smiled. 'Yes, Johnny writes stories and plays and poems. Maybe he can send you something one of these days, so that you can look at it? Would you do that?'

'Certainly,' I said. 'But I can only say what I think of anything he writes, I can't assess his talent. I can see whether you write well, Johnny, but not whether you will ever become a professional writer. We won't know about that until later.'

'I'll wait,' said Johnny quietly.

He's a good sort, I thought. Then I said, 'And when you're back in Kirchberg, Johnny, give my regards to everyone, especially Justus and No-Smoking!'

'You know them too?' asked Jonathan Trotz, puzzled. 'But who shall I say is sending his regards?'

'Their friend in Berlin,' I said. 'They'll know who that is. My regards to the boys as well.'

'Of course I'll tell them so. And will you send us your book when it's been printed?'

'I'll send it to Dr Bökh,' I said, 'and he can let the rest of you read it if he thinks that's the right thing to do. If not, then only Martin Thaler.'

So we said goodbye and shook hands. The captain and his foster-son walked on. Johnny turned back once to wave.

But now I must catch the Number One bus home, or the macaroni will get cold.

How surprised my mother will be when I tell her that I met Johnny Trotz and his captain!

Erich Kästner was born in Dresden in 1899. He began his career as a journalist for the *New Leipzig* newspaper in 1922, but moved to Berlin in 1927 to begin working as a freelance journalist and theatre critic. In 1929 he published his first book for children, *Emil and the Detectives*, which has since been translated into 60 languages, achieving international recognition and selling millions of copies around the world. He subsequently published both *Dot and Anton* and *The Flying Classroom*, before turning to adult fiction with his 1931 satire *Going to the Dogs*. After the Nazis took power in Germany, Kästner's books were burnt on Berlin's Opera Square and over the period of 1937-42 he faced repeated arrest and interrogation by the Gestapo, resulting in his blacklisting and exclusion from the writers' guild. After the end of World War II, Kästner moved to Munich and published *The Parent Trap*, later adapted into a hit film by Walt Disney. In 1957 he received the Georg Büchner Prize and, later, the Order of Merit and the prestigious Hans Christian Andersen Award for his contribution to children's literature. Kästner died in Munich in 1974.

Walter Trier was born in Prague in 1880. In 1910 he moved to Berlin, where he would later be introduced to Kästner, and began his career drawing cartoons for the *Berliner Illustrated*. He also contributed to the satirical weekly *Simplicissimus*, where during the 1920s, despite great personal risk, he ridiculed Hitler and the Nazi Party in a series of cartoons. In 1936 he fled to London, where he was involved in producing anti-Nazi leaflets and political propaganda drawings. He would go on to have a rich career, producing around 150 covers for the humorous magazine *Lilliput*. He died in 1951 in Ontario, Canada.

Anthea Bell is an award-winning translator. Having studied English at Oxford University, she has had a long and successful career, translating works from French, German and Danish. She is best known for her translations of the much-loved Asterix books, Stefan Zweig and W.G. Sebald.

PUSHKIN CHILDREN'S BOOKS

Just as we all are, children are fascinated by stories. From the earliest age, we love to hear about monsters and heroes, romance and death, disaster and rescue, from every place and time.

We created Pushkin Children's Books to share these tales from different languages and cultures with younger readers, and to open the door to the wide, colourful worlds these stories offer.

From picture books and adventure stories to fairy tales and classics, and from fifty-year-old bestsellers to current huge successes abroad, the books on the Pushkin Children's list reflect the very best stories from around the world, for our most discerning readers of all: children.